PU

SCARY TALES

TO TELL IN THE DARK

THERE ARE SIXTEEN OF THEM TOGETHER ON A

DARK WINTER'S NIGHT. EVERYONE SHOULD BE

ASLEEP, BUT THEN SOMEONE SAYS, 'LET'S TELL

GHOST STORIES.'

AND THAT'S JUST THE BEGINNING.

HERE ARE TEN TALES TO HAUNT YOU.

SCARY TALES

TO TELL IN THE DARK

ANTHONY MASTERS

PUFFIN BOOKS

PUFFIN BOOKS

Published by the Penguin Group
Penguin Books Ltd, 27 Wrights Lane, London W8 5TZ, England
Penguin Books USA Inc., 375 Hudson Street, New York, New York 10014, USA
Penguin Books Australia Ltd, Ringwood, Victoria, Australia
Penguin Books Canada Ltd, 10 Alcorn Avenue, Toronto, Ontario, Canada M4V 3B2
Penguin Books (NZ) Ltd, 182–190 Wairau Road, Auckland 10, New Zealand

Penguin Books Ltd, Registered Offices: Harmondsworth, Middlesex, England

Published in Puffin Books 1992
5 7 9 10 8 6

Typeset by DatIX International Limited, Bungay, Suffolk
Set in Monophoto Bembo
Printed in England by Clays Ltd, St Ives plc

To Robina, Mark, Vicky and Simon
with much, much love

CONTENTS

1 Nasty Nanny 13

2 Kelpie 26

3 Mountain Madness 40

4 The Wrong Bus..............54

5 The Ghost Mirrors..........67

6 Number Nine 84

7 The Green Man.............97

8 Time Trip 105

9 The Haunted Gondola....118

10 The Vampire...............127

The clock struck nine, the hollow booming echoing around the walls of the old mansion. Tim was sure he could hear something howling outside, but what could it be? It didn't sound like a dog and there weren't any wolves in England, were there?

It was Christmas Eve, and the sixteen of them were lying in sleeping-bags, warmed by the embers of the dying fire in the great hearth. Sometimes a spark soared up the chimney; occasionally there was a hiss as a splutter of flame was rekindled. In the distance they could all hear the adults enjoying themselves. There were the clink of glasses, the odd shout of laughter and the tinkling of the grand piano.

The house creaked and groaned in the rising wind like the timbers of an old ship. *It's almost as if it's alive,* thought Tim, and shivered. It wasn't the pleasantest of thoughts, but he also knew they were lucky to be here. Sometimes Christmas could be boring, with Dad asleep in his chair after lunch, Mum bad-tempered after cooking the turkey and Grandad telling his silly jokes. But this year, Lucy's parents had invited all their old friends (made over many years) and their children to an all-night party at Ramsden House. They were all together and they were going to have a wonderful time.

'Let's tell ghost stories,' said Lucy.

There was a gasp of nervous expectation.

'What a great idea,' whispered Tom.

'The scarier the better,' said someone Tim couldn't really identify in the dark.

'I'll start.' Lucy was firm. *Fair enough,* thought Tim. Ramsden House belonged to her parents, and there couldn't be a better background for a ghost story. It was a great barn of a place, standing in remote countryside on the edge of Exmoor, and with its towers and battlements and small latticed windows it looked like an old blind monster slumbering on the moorlands. They hadn't explored the inside properly yet, but Tim had already been knocked out by the sweeping staircase, the long, silent corridors and the minstrels' gallery overlooking the great hall with its rows of portraits of Lucy's ancestors. He was sure that the house must have secret rooms and at least one ghost.

'I'm going to tell a story about the house,' said Lucy, and Tim felt a wave of triumph. So he was right. This was going to be terrific. A rustle of anticipation went round every sleeping-bag as the charred logs in the fireplace snapped and groaned and Lucy began her story.

1

NASTY NANNY

I've had lots of nannies. It's not because my parents are
rich – they're not, and it's a big struggle to keep Ramsden House going – but because Dad's been away in the
army and Mum's been trying to open the house to
visitors, so it isn't possible for them to look after me all
the time. I've got a nice nanny now, Nanny Barlow –
she's downstairs at the party – but last year I had a really
nasty one. She was called Nanny Morris and she was
awful, but awful in a special way. It took me a while to
find that out, because at first she seemed quite kind.

I'll never forget the day she arrived. It was February
and really cold and blustery. I'd been waiting for her to
come, watching from the round window in my room
that overlooks the drive. It was late afternoon and the
light was just going and all the distances seemed funny.
You know what I mean – it's that time when you can't
quite see how near or far anything is. I'd wanted to see
her walking up the drive – that's how I check out all
nannies. You can often see what they're like just by the
way they walk. That little scurrying run with the head
down means she'll be nervous and anxious to please, so I
know I can boss her around all the time and get my
own way. The one in the big coat and boots with very
stiff shoulders is always more difficult; she'll definitely
shout a lot and expect her orders to be obeyed, so I'll
have to be careful and do things behind her back. Then
there's the tall, thin one who picks her feet up neatly; I

always know she's going to be fussy. But this one –
well, she wasn't like any of the others at all. She – she
kind of appeared half-way up the drive without me
seeing her, as if she'd just dropped out of the sky. One
moment the dead leaves were swirling up the gravel, the
next she was walking – well, more like gliding – up to
the front door. It was extraordinary, but I thought I
must have lost concentration or something.

She was very tall and skinny, and she wore this black
hat and coat and I couldn't hear her footsteps, even
when I opened the window. She looked up and I
honestly thought I could see the wind in her eyes; they
were all wild and milky and stary. It was weird.

She knocked at the door and Mum opened it. I crept
out into the corridor and heard them talking in the hall.
Their voices were very soft and it was almost as if they
were whispering. Then I realized that Mum had lowered
her voice because the new nanny kind of *breathed* her
words; it was strange to listen to, but once I'd got used
to it I could make out what she was saying all right.

'Well, I'm very pleased to meet you, Miss Morris.
Have you come far?'

'Far enough, my dear,' the new nanny replied mysteri-
ously.

Nervously, Mum rushed on. 'I know the agency
recommended you highly, but you've brought your
references, of course.'

'Here they are,' breathed Miss Morris. 'I think you'll
find them all in order.'

I could hear Mum riffling through them very quickly.
Then I heard her say, 'Well, they seem to be excellent. I
wasn't told you'd worked for someone like Lord Aber-
crombie.'

'Oh yes, an excellent gentleman.' She spoke a little
louder, as if she was making sure that Mum knew she

was in charge. 'Now, can I see my little girl?' Her voice was still low but sharp as a needle. A chill swept over me; I didn't like that voice one bit.

'Of course.' Mum seemed quite cowed and I could soon hear their shoes rapping up the sweeping wooden stairs. I hurried back into my bedroom and sat on the bed, feeling odd. Something strange was happening, but what was it? Or could it just be my imagination?

But when the door opened I felt even worse. The air in the room suddenly seemed much colder, and as Nanny Morris stood on the threshold in her long, dark clothes I was quite certain that she was – different.

'This is Miss Morris – the – your new nanny.' Mum stuttered and stumbled over her words, which is most unusual for her, and Nanny Morris smiled in a wintry way. Her face was very long and her nose was very sharp. In fact it was so sharp it was more like a beak than a nose. I stared at it, fascinated, the chill inside me spreading even further up my body.

'You look a nice little girl.' Her voice was like ice, but Mum didn't seem to notice. In fact she was looking much calmer now, as if she was sure that Nanny Morris and I were going to get along.

'Shall I leave you two alone?' she asked hopefully.

'Yes please,' replied Nanny Morris with a great big, cold smile that displayed two rows of huge, shiny, well-brushed, tombstone teeth. 'Then we can get to know each other, can't we, Lucy?'

I nodded dumbly, while inside my mind a voice screamed, *Who are you? What do you want?*

As soon as Mum had gone Nanny Morris's smile disappeared abruptly and she sat down heavily in a big basket chair, which creaked alarmingly. Then she kicked off her shoes to reveal some very large feet clad in black stockings. She wriggled her toes and sighed as if I wasn't there. After a while Nanny Morris spoke again. 'Well, Lucy?'

'Yes?'

'Are you going to be a good little girl?' There was a decided threat in her voice, which was low-pitched and still very cold.

I shivered. 'I hope so.'

'Because I'm going to teach you things. That's what I'm here for.'

I nodded obediently, wondering what she was going to teach me, because she hadn't been hired to give me lessons – just to look after me. After all, I went to St Elmers, like most of my friends.

Anyway, for a few days it was all a bit of a let-down, because although she stayed pretty weird nothing out of the ordinary happened. I went to school, came home, Nanny Morris got me my tea, supervised my homework and we would play cards before I went to bed. I even got used to her funny whispering sort of voice, and that long, pale face of hers.

She could be quite entertaining too. Before I went to sleep, she would sit on the edge of my bed and tell extraordinary stories of places where she had worked and people she had worked for: Crown princes and lords and ladies, dukes and sheikhs and even a Texan oil millionaire. I didn't really believe her but they were good stories – almost like fairy stories. One odd thing though: none of the stories ever really ended properly; they were always cut off, as if she had left the job she was in very abruptly.

However, as the days passed her stories changed; they didn't centre on all the people she'd worked for any more but were about how she'd walked in woods and old gardens, over moors and mountains, where she'd met gnomes and witches and trolls and hobgoblins. Of course, I knew she was making it all up, but her new stories were weird and frightening, about all the dark doings of the little people, and I found myself getting more and more scared. I think it was the look in her eyes that frightened me most; they were all smoky and misty, and when they rested on me I felt cold and had to snuggle right down in the bed and pull the blankets up hard. And the trouble was that once she'd left I felt she was still there, or at least her eyes were still coldly boring into me. I soon began to dream, and in my dreams I glimpsed the same mist that was in her eyes. Slowly it parted and I saw strange lands in which there were centaurs – half horse and half human – and pale gold unicorns and birds with crowns and beards and goblin-eating fish and fish-eating goblins and a desert full of trolls and mountain slopes running with honey and dark things on the peaks; things too horrible to think about.

One night, when both my parents were away for the first time and Nanny Morris and I were alone in the house, I felt more frightened than ever. I knew something special was up because her whispering voice seemed sharper and she kept smiling to herself as she prepared a special tea. There were four different kinds of sandwiches, doughnuts, biscuits, jam tarts and a huge fruit-cake.

I looked down at the feast suspiciously and then caught Nanny Morris's eye. Her face was still stretched in that fixed, secret smile and I knew I had to ask her.

'Nanny Morris –' I began.

'Yes, my dear.'

She'd never called me that before and the words had a strange ring to them. 'Er, is tonight special?'

'Yes, it's very special.' The whisper was pencil-sharp.

'Why?'

'We're celebrating.'

'Celebrating what?'

'I've finished my book,' she said triumphantly.

I stared at her, thoroughly mystified. 'What book?' I asked.

'It's my little secret. I've been writing a book. Sit down and eat up.'

'All right.' I did as she told me and attacked the delicious chunky sandwiches while she sank her big tombstone teeth into a doughnut. Bright-red jam spattered over her chin as she said, 'I'll read it to you later.'

'What's it about?' I asked, my mouth full. Normally Nanny Morris would have told me off, but she didn't seem to notice and was obviously intent on gorging herself on doughnuts.

'We'll go in the library later,' she said as if I hadn't spoken. 'That's the right place for reading books.'

'It'll be freezing in there,' I protested. The library is a big spooky room full of large, dusty, leather-bound volumes containing an army of marauding black spiders just watching their opportunity to scuttle up your arm. Yuk.

'I've lighted a fire,' she insisted. 'We'll have a nice cosy read.'

When we got down there, the library was in half-darkness, just lit by the flickering flames, and I could somehow feel the spiders everywhere, although I couldn't see them. Nanny Morris sat on a stool by the fire, her big bony knees making her skirt look like a twin-peaked mountainside, and pulled a book with a purple cover out of her old sewing-bag.

'You wrote *that*?'

'Yes.'

'What's it called?'

'It's called *Nanny's Dark Directory*.'

'Like a telephone directory?' I asked, puzzled.

'Not exactly, dear. It's more like a – a geography book. Now don't say any more – I'm going to read it to you and show you some pictures. Sit at my feet like a good girl.'

I caught a glimpse of spidery handwriting and brightly coloured pictures, but Nanny Morris held the book high above my head so I couldn't really see and began to read in her soft spider's-web of a voice.

'Dear Reader,' began Nanny Morris, 'let us take a magical journey to the dark lands where all the little folk – every troll and goblin, leprechaun and elf, imp and banshee, gnome and ghoul, hobgoblin and boggard, werewolf and fiend – are waiting to play with you. There are castles in the air and a cloud wilderness, marshes and swamps and a desert of magical dust. My will-o'-the-wisp will guide you through the dark lands. Look, Lucy, he's popped out of the book already. He *must* be keen.'

'What?'

'There – he's in the fireplace.'

I had the shock of my life when I gazed into the hearth, for just in front of the dancing flames was a little figure – more like a glow-worm than anything else, but with tiny hands and feet and a minute head that I could just make out. It – or he – or whatever – danced up and down on the ancient bricks. Was it just a spark from the coals, I wondered. But no, it was dancing towards us and stopped, poised on tiny feet, just in front of me, looking up with the most venomous pair of eyes I had ever seen in my life. They were red and bloodshot and flames seemed to leap behind the minute pupils. Its lips were parted in a snarl and its breath was like rotten fruit. I leapt to my feet with a scream, but Nanny Morris's strong, skeletal fingers were on my shoulders, forcing me to sit back down at her horny feet. Meanwhile the will-o'-the-wisp gave a horrible, jarring, metallic laugh and smoke came out of its ears.

'Stay there,' Nanny Morris snapped. 'Don't move.'

'What are you doing?' I yelled.

'I'm releasing my prisoners,' she said, and laughed in the same horrible metallic way as the will-o'-the-wisp had. It was like the scraping of a chair across the floor or the sound of a skewer running down a blackboard.

'You're a witch, aren't you?' I said suddenly, and this time the by now familiar chill flooded right over me.

She nodded. 'I come from a coven that's able to penetrate the dark lands.' Her voice was as cold and menacing as an Arctic night.

'What do you want with me?'

'No one believes in fairies any more,' she said. 'So none of the dark lands' creatures can haunt anyone now. But I had this brilliant idea, and on my last visit I caught some and captured them in my book. Now I can start releasing them and people are bound to believe in what they *see*, aren't they?' She laughed silkily.

'How are you going to release them then?' I asked, trembling all over but determined not to give in completely.

'It's not been easy,' she confided. 'I've been nanny to child after child and do you know what, Lucy?'

'What?'

'None of them had any imagination – not like you.' Somehow she made the compliment seem the most threatening thing I had ever heard.

'But did they *need* any?' I asked crossly. 'You said these creatures really existed.'

'They do.' She wrinkled up her long, sharp nose. 'But they have to be *summoned up*, by the imagination. And do you know, you're the first little girl I've come across so far who's got one. I mean, look at that will-o'-the-wisp.'

As she spoke the will-o'-the-wisp danced up to me again and spat, and the spittle ran down my jeans, smelling of vinegar. Then he laughed his metallic laugh again and danced back into the hearth.

'So, as I say, I'm able to release my prisoners, for their own good. They should be very grateful to me, in the end.'

'And what about *me*?' I asked indignantly.

'Oh, you'll be all right. They won't all stay *here*, you know. They'll want to *explore*.'

I shuddered, trying not to think about the creatures of the dark lands and what they might do to my family and my home, in case by doing so I released them from Nanny Morris's book.

'Nanny Morris?' I said at last.

'Yes, my dear?'

'What would put them back in your book? What would make you have to kidnap them all over again – and take them back to the dark lands?'

She laughed uproariously, as if I had made a very good joke, and the will-o'-the-wisp spluttered out more vinegar and clapped its tiny, scaly hands together with a sound like old, dry, cracked leather.

'The only thing that would force me to collect them up again is if people weren't frightened of them, and that's not very likely, is it? Watch out – there's another one coming.'

Over the top of the book a truly dreadful apparition peered out and I screamed again and again and again. What was it? I can only vaguely remember now. It had the head of a rat, the face of an old man and instead of a nose it had a wriggling worm. The thing winked at me, leering with its wizened little blackcurrant eyes.

'Now look what you've summoned up,' cackled Nanny Morris. 'But I'm sure your imagination can release some even nastier things than that.'

The creature disappeared behind the page. 'What was it?' I whispered.

'Hobgoblin,' she replied. 'Rat-head type – usually found in the Fanged Forest. I had quite a time collecting him.'

I nodded. I was sure she had.

Then something scuttled behind me, something that sounded as if it had a good number of legs. I didn't dare to look round. Suddenly I caught sight of a scaly tail swinging behind a picture, and although I tried to glance away I saw a bloated face with four eyes, two mouths and what looked like another eye on top of its head. All were swivelling wildly.

'Boggard,' said Nanny Morris gleefully. 'Caught in the Yellow Swamp.'

'I'm going to bed,' I said, determined not to allow any more of these horrors out of the pages of the book.

'Sweet dreams.' She smiled.

I hurried out of the library, knowing that it was all only just beginning. The blood pounded in my head and I was shivering all over, but when I reached my room all was as usual and gradually the trembling began to stop. Maybe they weren't as powerful as she said; maybe I didn't have as much imagination as she thought – either way I was silently relieved, and the longer I just sat quietly on the bed, the more relaxed I felt.

Ten minutes later I was still sitting there, feeling better and better. Possibly the creatures and the book didn't exist at all. Had Nanny Morris hypnotized me in some way just to give me a scare? Well, my parents would be home in the morning and I'd tell them. Then they would sack her, and good riddance.

I yawned, undressed and put on my pyjamas. It would be lovely in bed, warm and comfortable, and I would be able to forget this living nightmare. But when I twitched back the duvet, the scream bubbled up into my throat.

There were six of them, small gnomes with entwined tails and black, hairy faces. They were lying on the pillow, making a terrible grinding noise with their teeth, and the smell was awful. Then suddenly I heard a whirring sound, rather like a broken clockwork mouse, and out from underneath the bed slipped a banshee and a ghoul. I can't tell you which was the more foul, but they were hand in hand, grinning as if I was going to like what I saw.

'Go away,' I said feebly, but they advanced on me instead, while the miniature gnomes on the pillow continued to grind their teeth. '*Go away!*' I yelled, but they continued advancing on me until I was giving out little yelps of fear. I had tucked myself under the windowsill, but they kept on coming, the banshee all wavy and wafty with no lips and blackened teeth, and the ghoul dead white with a long face and great darting eyes. Its tongue kept flicking out towards me, like a snake, and there was something on the tip of it. Then I saw that it was a very large, black, leggy spider that looked poised to spring.

I wasn't screaming now, just whimpering somewhere deep down, and I knew I was going to be sick. A small, scruffy elf with a dirty face and tousled hair was swinging on my favourite picture of my parents. Then the picture string broke and the elf and the frame plunged down in a wreckage of smashing glass.

In my desperation an idea came to me. Suppose, just suppose, I could destroy Nanny Morris's directory. Would there be a chance then of all its recently released captives being returned to where they came from? It was an outside chance, but I had to take the risk.

I pounded down the great staircase towards the library, but as I reached the foot of the stairs, I was greeted by the most amazing sight: the whole of the hallway was filled with flying, gibbering, hideous little creatures from the dark lands, all waving and grunting and calling to me at the same time.

I wrenched open the library door to see dozens of weird and terrifying creatures filling the room, standing, crouching, flying, crawling in a semicircle around Nanny Morris. I could see her large feet, long black skirt, powerful arms – but her head was no longer there. Instead she had the head of a huge goblin with protruding eyes and hard lips that looked as if they had been made out of dead wood.

Instinctively I ran for the book and, taking the goblin off guard, I snatched the directory out of its horny hands. With a cry of triumph I pushed the goblin away and threw the book into the flames. Somehow I knew this was the right thing to do, for at least I had deprived the inhabitants of the dark lands of their means of transport. But I hadn't realized I'd also deprived them of a home, of their very existence – for there came a series of wild shrieks and guttural cries as the creatures began to shrivel up, just as though they themselves were burning. In a very short time they were dried husks lying on the floor and soon they were dust, blown hither and thither in the draught from the long library windows. When I looked up, I saw Nanny Morris's goblin head was growing larger and larger by the second.

'You'll pay for this,' she screamed as she watched the directory burning in the roaring fire

Then, to my horror and amazement, her pumpkin-like head exploded and the flames leapt out from the fire and seized Nanny Morris's body. In seconds she melted before my eyes to a pool of oily water on the library carpet. Then the pool evaporated and there was nothing there at all to show that she had ever existed.

Lucy walked through the firelit shadows to a desk. She opened it and rummaged in a drawer. Then she brought out a small, flat box and opened it.

'*What's in there?*' *asked Roger.*

'*It's the front cover —*' *began Annie.*

'*Of a book,*' *said Lucy as she held it up.*

They all stared hard at the partly burnt binding. Then Roger slowly read: '*Nanny's Dark Directory*'.

'*I thought I'd keep it as a souvenir,*' *said Lucy quietly.*

'*I've got the next one,*' *said Derek.* '*It's a bit out in the wilds, right out in Shetland in fact.*'

2

KELPIE

It all started when George disappeared from an island off Shetland. Everyone thought he'd drowned, until the message in the whisky bottle was washed up on the beach; the sea is very wild and treacherous round that coast and it's easy to get cut off by the tide. But the writing was clearly George's, although no one could understand the message at all. Written on a scrap of paper from his Filofax, it read: *It's started. God help me. I know* . . . Then the writing faded away into a scrawl and petered out. There weren't any other clues at all.

George was a TV producer and he was my dad's best friend. We've got this farm in Devon and George and his daughter Becky always used to come for their summer holidays. His wife had walked out on him years ago and he'd brought Becky up on his own. They were devoted to one another, and when George disappeared, Becky came to live with us. It was a real tragedy. Becky was heart-broken, and although we tried to look after her as best we could, I thought she'd never stop being unhappy.

But it was Dad as well as Becky who really worried me and Mum. He and George had been childhood friends and I knew they were very close, but ever since the bottle had been washed up on the beach, about two weeks after George's disappearance, Dad had been acting strangely. Apart from being grief-stricken, there was something else – a peculiar restlessness about him. He went for long walks, was very silent, and kept sitting on his own, as if he was trying to puzzle something out.

Then one September evening he said to us all at supper, 'I'm going up to Shetland.'

'Why?' asked Mum, looking very worried.

'There are some things about George's death I'm not satisfied about.'

'What things?' said Becky. But she looked more hopeful than afraid, as if any new information about her father might somehow keep his memory more alive.

'Just things,' he said vaguely. Dad could be like that; he was one of those people very much in touch with the earth, as if the fields and the trees and the wind gave him a special knowledge. He'd never done anything other than farming, and his father before him, and *his* father before *him* – and so on. It went right back in the family for hundreds of years. I saw Mum looking at Dad in that special way of hers; she knew and understood him better than anyone.

'I want to go with you,' said Becky suddenly, with characteristic determination. She was just like her father in that way. Once she had decided to do something, she had decided to do it, and that was that.

'Then I'm going too,' I insisted.

'You'll miss school,' Dad protested.

'Great,' I replied.

'I think you should all go,' said Mum slowly, and I knew she felt it would do Becky good – help her come to terms with her father's death – and anyway, once my dad had had one of his hunches there was no stopping him. He'd done it before. For instance, he had been certain that the tide would breach the sea wall at Breakmouth – had tried and tried to get it strengthened – and was still arguing with the council when the sea broke through. They were all very sheepish about it. Dad had

had another of his hunches about an old abandoned quarry, used as an unofficial children's playground. He was suddenly quite sure that the sides were unsafe. Sure enough, one of them caved in and it was only luck that saved the children there. So we all took Dad's hunches very seriously.

'You three go – and I'll look after the farm,' volunteered Mum, and Dad smiled at her gratefully.

'We shan't be gone long,' he promised. 'Just for a few days. It won't take much time for me to –' and his voice had died away in that irritating way it had when he was concealing an unthought-out theory.

George had been up in Shetland doing some research on one of his TV programmes. They were usually terrific; often about creatures in some far-away place – mysterious and haunting. He'd done programmes about sharks on a Pacific reef, elephants in the depths of Africa, wild dogs in Australia and some strange little hummingbirds in Paraguay. But no one, not even Becky, had really known what he had been doing in Shetland.

'Something about seals,' she had told me. 'But he was very secretive about it – which is pretty odd. I mean, he's not usually like that. And, Derek – I know he's still there. I can *feel* him.'

I wondered if she'd got my father's gift of 'hunches' but I didn't really know, so I had mixed feelings about the trip to Shetland, which is one big island and lots of little ones off the east coast of Scotland. I was partly glad to be going because I thought the journey might help Becky – even if it was a sad one – but I also wanted to go because I had loved George dearly. Apart from being a really exciting person, he was a very kind one, and I knew that he had been fond of us all.

We flew to Aberdeen and then on a propeller aircraft to

Lerwick. Directly we arrived on Shetland I knew we were in a wilderness. There were hardly any trees, just mile after mile of wind-blown open land with lochs and mysterious ruins and great craggy cliffs soaring up above a lashing sea.

From Shetland we went in a ferry to Sula, a tiny uninhabited island just off the coast – uninhabited except for Macleish, a hermit who lived in a ramshackle cottage practically on the beach of a small bay. He had allowed George to put up a tent on the spiky grass on a ridge behind his house, and he was going to allow the three of us to do the same. All this had been organized by a hotel owner on the mainland who knew Macleish and had this to say about him: 'We don't even know his first name – no one does; he's been on Sula for years, entirely on his own. Weird old man. Hardly speaks and roams the island day and night. He's got a few sheep. Does a bit of fishing and grows a few potatoes. Completely self-sufficient. Wouldn't say a word about George's disappearance.'

Once the ferry left we all felt a bit lost, as if we shouldn't be there. Like Dad, I was used to the sounds of the countryside at night, but this was different. The sighing of the waves on the rocks, the shriek of the gulls, the roaring of the sea in a cave, the whining of the coming night wind, all made me feel unwanted, as if we were trespassing.

Dad went and knocked on Macleish's battered old wooden door and Becky and I waited anxiously, wondering if he would be unfriendly or even aggressive. But instead, when he had withdrawn an amazing number of bolts and opened the door, Macleish turned out to be a very fragile old man with rheumy eyes and long, lank, snow-white hair. He looks a bit like a ragged old sea-gull, I thought, and for that reason he made me shudder.

His hands and face looked clammy, as if he was running a fever; there was perspiration on his forehead despite the chill of the night air.

'What do you want?' His accent was broad but he enunciated the words very precisely, as if he was speaking to three foreigners and was determined that they should understand him.

'You said – the hotel said –' Dad began to muddle up his words, as he often did when he was nervous. I could have screamed because the old man stared at him as if he was barmy, and I could feel Becky getting very tense beside me. 'The Glen Hotel – Mr Ferguson – he said you wouldn't mind if I put up a tent.'

'Eh?'

'A tent. We want to put up a tent.'

'Whatever for?'

'It's rather windy,' said Becky. 'We've got to sleep somewhere.'

'Aye.' He seemed to see the reason for the tent at last. 'Well . . . you'll put it behind the house where Mr Patrick had his. Poor devil.'

'He's my father. What happened to him?' Becky's voice trembled and I really admired her for the way she spoke up. It took guts.

'The sea took him.'

'Just like that?' asked Dad.

'What do you mean?' Macleish gazed at him quizzically.

'Do you know any more?' translated Becky.

Macleish turned to her and smiled gently. He seemed to be much more at ease with her. 'It's a wicked coast.'

'Did you *see* anything?' she insisted. Again there was that slight tremble in her voice, but the old man didn't seem to notice.

'What should I have seen?'

'Anything strange.'

'There are many strange things,' he said. 'Particularly on Sula.'

'What sort of things?' She was very persistent.

'Legends. Myths. The Norsemen were here, you know, with their magic. But there's old magic too.' He seemed to be speaking only for her, totally ignoring Dad and me as if we'd suddenly stopped existing.

'What sort of old magic?'

'Kelpies. The seal people. They're here, you know. That's what your father came about. It was a mistake.' His voice died away.

'Why?' Becky was still persistent.

'You mustn't look. If you do –'

'Look at what?'

'The kelpie.' He cleared his throat as the wind got up. 'Away and pitch your tent,' he said dismissively. 'Go and get under cover. I don't like the wind.'

'Don't *like* it?' I said, speaking for the first time.

'It's a kelpie wind,' he replied, and slammed the wooden door shut in our faces.

We pitched the tent with some difficulty in the gusty weather and tried to make ourselves comfortable inside it. Above the wind there was a new sound – a kind of hollow booming.

'The sea comes in underneath us somewhere,' said Dad, trying to boil a kettle under the awning. I shivered; it was frightening to think of the thousands of tonnes of churning water thundering about below us. I imagined being trapped in a cave, caught by the tide, waiting to drown. Had something like that happened to George? I looked across the shadowed walls of the tent at Becky, wondering if she was thinking the same thing, but she was sitting with her knees drawn up to her chin, her head down, and I couldn't see her expression.

Suddenly she stiffened and looked up. 'What's that?'

I tried to listen but all I could hear was the booming. 'I can't hear anything.'

'Listen.' She was absolutely rigid and I wondered if she was ill. 'They're calling,' she said.

'Who are?' For a moment I thought she must have been asleep, but when I saw her eyes so wide and intent I decided that she hadn't.

'What's up?' asked Dad, peering into the tent as he poured out the tea at last and opened up packets of rather battered-looking sandwiches.

'Becky's heard something –'

'The sea,' he muttered.

'No,' I replied, staring at Becky in concern. 'It was something else.' There was a light in her eye that was unearthly, horrible, inhuman, and I stood up, bumping my head against a tent-pole.

She looked up at me and smiled. 'Now you can hear it, Derek.' Her voice was barely recognizable – a hoarse half-whisper that was deep and animal-like.

Appalled, I was about to call out to Dad when I heard it – a cry that came from beneath us, a cry that really terrified me. There was definitely something human in it, but not much; the rest was a haunting, animal-like yearning, and when I looked at Becky my terror grew, for she was half-crouched, her eyes filled with longing. Then she, too, made the cry, which seemed much more despairing, much more fearful.

'What the hell was that?' asked Dad, blundering into the tent and sending a couple of rucksacks flying.

'It's Becky. She's ill.'

'Becky –' But she had her hands up and her teeth gleamed in the darkness.

'Kall Kallandis.' Now she was talking gibberish, but it was gibberish in a hard, grating language that once again was not entirely human. 'Kall Kallandis,' she yelled. 'Kallandis Raman.'

As Dad and I stood there, gazing at Becky in amazement, the tent flap was pushed aside and I saw the mad eyes of Macleish, his face chalk-white in the bright moonlight. 'Who gives the call?' he cried.

Dad whirled round. 'I don't know what you're talking about. Becky – she's ill. Not herself.'

'She gave the call.'

'*What* call?' yelled Dad.

'The kelpie. The call of the kelpie.'

'What rubbish!'

I turned back to her, and cried out in fear, for Becky was gazing up at Macleish in a strange kind of awe and wonderment and her beautiful big eyes were shining with joy. 'Raman,' she shouted. 'Master.'

Macleish smiled and withdrew his head, his hand pushing back the flap.

'Wait!' yelled Dad. 'Wait – Macleish –'

'Becky,' I whispered. 'Are you all right?' My mind partly registered that she was looking more normal, that the terrible light had gone out of her eyes, but another fear had suddenly assaulted me with such force that I could barely take in anything else. 'Dad –' I began, realizing what I had just seen.

'That old fool.' He was gathering up Becky in his arms, patting her lovingly as she snuggled into his oilskin coat. 'He's crazy. Not safe to be around. Talking all that –'

'*Dad!*'

'Yes?'

'Did you see his hands?'

'What about them?'

'They were covered with fur,' I whispered.

'*What?*'

'His hands – the tops were all covered in fur.'

Somehow we got the sandwiches down and clambered into the sleeping-bags. Becky seemed fine now, unconscious of what she had said or of Macleish's appearance. What was more, Dad seemed totally uninterested in the state of the old man's hands.

'We *must* get some sleep,' he said, and he sounded so angry that I knew I shouldn't – couldn't argue with him. Dad is the kind of person who is so used to giving instructions and expecting them to be obeyed that there was no point in resisting him. Anyway, I was sure that in the morning, when it was daylight, a very obvious explanation would be found for everything.

But morning didn't come for a very long time, and I lay in the semi-darkness of the tent hearing the booming beneath me and pulling my sleeping-bag up round my ears. The wind cried and moaned outside but never reached full gale force, and thanks to Dad's careful pegging the tent remained stable.

Outside there was a full moon and the pallid light came into the tent in a faint glow, picking out the outlines of the sleeping-bags and the rucksacks. It wasn't exactly cold, but I felt chilled and very uneasy as I lay there with the moonlight filling up the tent more and more until I felt as if I was bathed in it.

I half slept then woke up with a jerk, knowing something was wrong but not immediately able to decide what it was. My eyes roved round the tent. Well, we were all here and nothing was missing. Then my eyes alighted on Becky's hands, which were clasped in front of her, resting on the top of her sleeping-bag. Both her wrists and the top of her hands were covered in smooth, brown fur.

'Becky,' I whispered.

She didn't reply.

'Becky —' She sat up, raised one of her fur-covered hands and hit me so hard across the forehead that I fell back, seeing stars and then watching a long, dark tunnel of blackness rush towards me.

I woke up, not sure of the passing of time. My face was aching and it took me a few seconds to realize what had happened. With a sense of shock I pulled myself up and stared around the moon-washed interior of the tent. My father lay there, sleeping peacefully, his chest rising and falling evenly, but of Becky there was no sign whatsoever.

'Becky!'

My father woke. 'What's happened?'

'Becky's gone.'

'Maybe she went out for a pee,' he grunted.

'If she did, she hit me first.'

'What?'

'She knocked me out,' I protested indignantly.

'Don't be ridiculous.'

'It feels terrible. Just take a look at it, would you?'

Dad flashed the torch at my face and whistled. 'Blimey — that's a real shiner.'

'Thanks.'

'What were you two fighting about then?' he asked brusquely.

'We weren't fighting about anything — she just hit me.'

'But what *for*?'

'She had fur on her hands.'

He was silent and I didn't know whether he believed me or not. 'Come on. We'd better see where she is,' he said at last. 'You OK to come?'

'You bet.' I wriggled out of my bag and followed him outside. It was light now and we could both see very clearly where we were going, but there was no sign of Becky and the hollow booming sound below our feet seemed louder.

'Where the hell can she be?' asked Dad, looking really worried.

'What's that?' I said sharply, pointing to a dark hump in the grass.

'It's a sheep.'

'No, it's too long. It's kind of – kind of lolling there,' I said, feeling inadequate, unable to describe what looked to me like a dark cylindrical shape which wasn't quite cylindrical. Then I gave a little yelp of shock and surprise. The shape wasn't quite cylindrical because it had a human head which was waving to and fro.

I think Dad noticed it at the same time for he suddenly moved in front of me.

'Come on, Dad. Let's take a look.'

'We don't know what it is.' He hesitated.

'We never will unless we check it out,' I said impatiently, acutely aware that neither of us could say what we thought we'd seen.

'OK, but stay behind me.'

'All right.' I was deeply afraid, but my curiosity was stronger, and somehow the fact that Dad was there made it all right. Whatever it was, Dad would sort it out.

'Now what?' I said as he paused.

'Stop.'

'Dad –'

'Don't move!'

'What is it?'

'It can't be,' he muttered, grabbing me to him and blocking my view.

'What *is* it?' I couldn't bear the agony of the suspense any longer and broke away from him. Then I gave a gasp of revulsion. Lying on the grass was a wet, dark seal, but its head belonged to Macleish.

The head turned and spoke throatily in a blurred sort of way.

'It came to me. It came to me too early.'

'What's happened to you?' I whispered.

'Kelpie wind.'

'You're a seal.' I wondered if I was dreaming or going mad, and looking at Dad I could see he was completely stunned.

'I ran for the beach. It was too late.'

'You mean you changed —' It was unbelievable.

'Help me.' His voice was bubbly now, and some enormous change was taking place, for the human features were distorting, shifting, changing. Seconds later, a seal's head looked plaintively up at me and from deep in its throat a swallowed human voice screamed, 'Get me to the beach, or I'll die.' Then the voice went altogether, to be replaced by a guttural call that chilled me to the bone.

Dad spoke for the first time. 'Becky. Where is she?'

I remembered the fur on her hands. 'She's changing, Dad,' I said mechanically, too shocked to feel any emotion.

'What?'

'She's gone to join George — gone to join her father.' Suddenly I knew instinctively what had happened. 'George — he's a kelpie. Like her. Like Macleish — like anyone might be who comes to this island at the wrong time. Look down there. *Look.*'

The sun was rising now and picking out the white foam of the shallows. There, frolicking in the waves, were two seals, a large one and a smaller one. George and Becky.

'Anyone who comes to the island at the wrong time,' repeated my father woodenly. 'What did Macleish say about the wind? Don't you mean anyone who stays on the island for a certain length of time – maybe a night – when the kelpie wind is blowing?'

I froze. 'What are you saying, Dad?'

'Look at the back of your hands, son.'

I couldn't. I couldn't look down at them.

'Look at the back of your hands,' insisted Dad.

Slowly, unwillingly, I looked. 'They're all right,' I cried. 'We mustn't let it get to us.'

'We've got to get away.' There was panic in his eyes and I suddenly felt old, old enough to be *his* father.

The seal that was Macleish made a pitiful mewing sound and we both jumped, our nerves in tatters.

'We can't leave him here,' I said. 'He'll die.'

'All right – we'll get him down to the beach. Then we must find his boat and row – row away – fast.'

'What about Becky?' I said slowly.

'She's gone. She's changed. Come on!' he rapped out impatiently. 'Time's running out.'

Somehow we managed to grab the seal, and between us half-drag, half-carry it down to the beach. But all the time I was sure the fur must be growing on my hands, and was terrified that we would be too late.

Derek held up his hands in the firelight and everyone looked at them closely. There didn't seem to be any fur on them. Yet. There was a long silence and then Liz said, 'Let's hear another story. I've got one. It's called "Mountain Madness".' She paused and gulped. 'Oh dear.'

'What's the matter?' asked Tim.

'It all happened when my brother Jake and I went skiing last year.'

'You can't tell that one,' said a muffled voice. 'It's horrible.'

'It may be horrible,' she snapped, 'but it really happened, and if we tell it, it'll make us feel better.'

'Will it?' said Jake.

3

MOUNTAIN MADNESS

We were having a skiing holiday with our parents in Bulgaria. There was a good lot of snow last year and, because Jake and I have been skiing with the family since we were very tiny and are really good skiers, we were often allowed out on the slopes on our own. Anyway, we had this ski lodge high up on the mountain and late one afternoon, when it was nearly dark, Jake and I were making our way back across country and by mistake ski'd into a valley we hadn't been to before. The stars were just coming out, little pinpricks of light above us, and we had never felt so fit and happy.

Jake saw the castle first, rearing up above the valley. The light was blazing from the windows and we could hear the sound of distant music.

'They must be having a party,' I said. 'Let's go and have a look.' Jake agreed at once. He used to be very adventurous – but not any more.

We ski'd over and went to take a closer look. It really was the most beautiful castle – all turrets and towers and an ornate drawbridge. Even from a distance we could see that the dance was obviously very grand, and there was a full orchestra. Couples were dancing and they wore the most beautiful, elegant clothes I've ever seen. It all looked magnificent, but I suddenly had a sinking inner feeling that there was something wrong, although for a few seconds I couldn't work out what it was.

'They're not human,' said Jake suddenly, and I felt my stomach muscles clench with fright.

'*What?*'

'Look for yourself. They're not human at all. None of them are.'

I stared more intently, and as one of the guests passed close to the window I recoiled with shock: his head was clearly, unmistakably, the head of a wolf.

'I don't believe it,' I muttered. Then the obvious explanation occurred to me. 'Of course, they're wearing masks, aren't they?'

'Pretty realistic masks. And what about their hands?'

I took a closer look at a pair of stylishly twirling dancers. Sure enough, their interlocked hands were definitely covered with fur. Could they be gloves? Could this be the most dressed-up fancy-dress party of all time?

Suddenly the music ended and this was greeted with snarls and howls of disapproval. Jake and I shuddered. There was something unearthly, terrifying, in the sound.

'Blimey,' I whispered. 'What on earth do you make of this?'

'Let's go,' said Jake fearfully.

'Go?' I replied indignantly. 'Go, when we've discovered a genuine fairy-tale palace?'

'What are you going to do then?' he snapped sarcastically. 'Join them?'

I could see that Jake was petrified and that I was probably being stupid, but the glittering, sinister scene had already bewitched me and I didn't want to leave. Wild thoughts were rushing through my mind. Could it be some beautifully mounted fake? Would the guests soon peel off masks and gloves to reveal human faces and lily-white skin beneath?

'Wait.' Jake grabbed my arm as I was about to edge in closer. 'Don't move.'

'What's the matter?' My fascination was beginning to turn to fear.

'Look!'

I started to tremble as I saw what Jake was silently pointing at. Two wolves, unclothed dark shadows, were padding towards the drawbridge of the castle. They trotted silently across the snow-covered bridge and then one of them sprang up and pulled at an overhanging chain with its paw. A long, mournful note began to sound and the massive iron-studded door swung slowly open. A wolf servant stood there in the finest livery. He bowed and the two wolves slowly padded in, the great door clanging to behind them.

'Wow!' Jake seemed more confident now. 'It's amazing.'

It certainly was, I thought, as I looked high up the castle walls. 'Wait —' I said. 'Look up there.' The window at the top of one of the towers was barred, but it was brightly lit and there was a shape moving about.

'It's not a wolf,' said Jake encouragingly.

'No. It's an old lady. I think she's seen us,' I said panicking.

'How can she have? It's dark out here.'

'Well, it looks as if she has. She's holding something up against the bars.'

'It's a baby,' said Jake. 'I can see it clearly. It's an ordinary baby.'

It was hard to make out anything of the old lady's expression, but somehow the way her arms were thrust out, holding up the baby behind the bars, seemed to indicate that she was desperate. But why was she so desperate, I wondered. Was she a prisoner? Who did the baby belong to?

'What shall we do?' I asked Jake.

'Go home,' he said without any hesitation.

'But we can't just –'

'Come on. It feels bad here.'

'Feels bad? I don't know what you mean.'

'It just does.'

And suddenly I knew what he meant. There was a greater chill in the air, a wildness to the dancing, a stamping of paws – and was that a wolf's eye watching us through a downstairs window? But upstairs? She was still there, holding the baby up more imploringly than ever, and I felt that the baby's eyes were on mine, burning into me.

'OK,' I whispered. 'Let's go.'

We ski'd away swiftly from the chill image of that place, and with a tremendous sense of relief soon found ourselves back on the familiar slopes again. As we drew up outside the ski lodge I said vehemently, 'We've got to go back there.'

'No way.'

'By day.'

'Not a chance.'

'With Mum and Dad? It'll be all right – and I remember the way.'

'So do I,' said Jake slowly. 'But so what? You won't catch me going back there again.'

The next day we ski'd back to the little valley with Mum and Dad. We had argued about it for hours and finally agreed to tell them about the castle but not about the wolves or the old lady and the baby.

I was dying to go back and check that we hadn't somehow imagined it all, but as we neared the valley, even in broad daylight under a sparkling morning sun, I still felt scared and I knew that poor Jake did too. We ski'd on until we came to the sharp dip into the valley. Once we were there I looked up to see the soaring cliff.

It was there all right, but there was no castle built into it – just a bare, icy crag.

'Where is it?' asked Jake angrily.

I stared around me at the snow-capped mountains. There was not the hint of a castle anywhere.

'Maybe you got the wrong valley,' said Dad.

'No,' I snapped. 'I'm certain this is the place. Aren't you, Jake?'

'Yeah. But there's no castle,' he said flatly.

I saw Dad and Mum exchange glances. I knew what they were thinking – that we had imagined it all.

'Mum – it was here.'

'Yes, darling.'

'You don't believe me, do you?' I yelled.

'Yes,' said Dad. 'I believe you both saw it.'

'You do?' said Jake, amazed.

'Sure – but I have to tell you the castle was nothing more than an illusion.'

'How do you make *that* out?' I asked crossly.

'Mountain madness,' chuckled Dad.

'What?' asked Jake suspiciously.

'Snow-blindness – makes you have all kinds of hallucinations. It's all that white. Anyone could see castles in the air.'

'But there were wolves dancing, weren't there, Jake?' I blurted out.

He nodded reluctantly.

'And an old lady with a baby. She was a prisoner or something.'

Jake nodded again, looking very unhappy indeed.

'That's what I mean,' said Dad. 'Maybe you two have been doing too much skiing.' He turned to Mum. 'I think we should spend the rest of the day in the city. There's some Roman ruins we haven't seen and –'

'Ruins –' Jake and I moaned. 'Not ruins.'

'Yes,' said Mum firmly. 'It's time for a change of scene.'

We weren't allowed back on the slopes for another day, and even then it was only after endless discussion about wearing snow-goggles all the time and not going too far.

Eventually we managed to get permission to go out for a short ski, and Dad even joked, 'Watch out for those dancing wolves.' It was just too humiliating.

'We're going back there, aren't we?' said Jake gloomily.

'Yes,' I said fiercely.

We ski'd back towards the valley and as we went, our uneasiness grew. I knew that Jake was terrified and that I was forcing him on, but I felt we had to go back for the baby's sake if no one else's.

'You scared?' I asked Jake.

'You bet.'

We arrived in the valley just as the light was fading and, for a moment, as we ski'd down the sharp descent, I thought the castle wasn't there and that Mum and Dad had been right all along. But then we both saw it — brightly lit and as fairy-tale-like as before. This time, however, there was no music and no dancing and, as far as we could see, no wolves.

'Why should the castle be all lit up,' asked Jake anxiously, 'when no one's there and nothing's happening?'

'Wait,' I said. 'Look up there.'

The old lady was there again, holding the baby aloft in the upstairs window, looking as desperate as before.

Then Jake said, 'The door's opening.'

But there was no servant there — just an empty space slowly being revealed as the great iron-studded door slowly and soundlessly swung open.

'It's a trap,' whispered Jake.

It certainly didn't look good, I thought, staring up again at the old woman. This time there was no doubt that she could see us; in fact, she was actually beckoning urgently, her face miserable and imploring. Then the baby began to cry.

'No,' said Jake, 'we can't.'

'It looks empty.'

'No –'

'Come on. Let's just have a peek round the door.'

'That's all then.'

'OK.'

We took off our skis and hid them in the bushes. Then we hurried over the drawbridge, our footsteps making no sound at all. There had been a fresh fall of snow that morning and there were no other footprints, which seemed a good sign. Of course, I told myself, they could all be hiding inside, and I knew that was exactly what Jake was thinking.

The door was half-open.

'Take a look then,' I said sharply, suddenly losing my nerve.

'All right,' he said uneasily. He poked his head round and then withdrew it quickly. 'Blimey.'

'What's up?'

'It's cold in there.'

'Yes, but is anyone *there*?' I asked him impatiently.

'No.'

'You sure?'

'I'm sure.'

'Come on then.' I pushed past him but Jake grabbed my arm.

'Wait.'

'What for?'

'We really shouldn't go in.' He sounded terrified and I saw that he was shaking.

'Think of the old woman and the baby,' I said. 'They need rescuing.'

'You sure?'

'It's obvious.'

I stepped through the door and Jake reluctantly followed.

It was certainly very cold in the hallway of the castle – much colder than it was outside in the snow. There were no paintings on the walls, and not a stick of furniture anywhere. Stalactites hung from the shadowed ceiling and ahead of us we could see the dim outline of a magnificent staircase.

'Let's go straight up the stairs,' I said.

We ran as lightly as we could in order to make as little noise as possible. As we passed the other rooms, we could see through their open doors that they were completely empty and all the rich furnishings had gone.

The staircase wound up and up and we both knew we had to continue right to the top of the castle. Floor after floor branched off – linked by gloomy corridors with icicle-hung ceilings – but finally we reached the very top.

'Listen,' said Jake, and sure enough we could hear a baby crying.

'It's this way,' I said.

'OK.'

We walked slowly and quietly down the stone corridor towards the sounds of crying. Eventually the corridor began to narrow, until we were practically squeezing our way along between the ice-cold walls.

'Why's it like this?' I hissed at Jake.

'I don't know. Maybe it's the servants' quarters.'

'Very thin servants,' I muttered, as the walls became narrower and even icier.

47

'No central heating either,' shivered Jake. Then we stopped dead, for the cries of the baby were just around the corner.

'OK,' said Jake. 'We'll have to help them now we've come so far.'

We inched forward to find a sliding door that was already half-open. Inside was the old lady with white hair and a peach-like complexion. In her arms she was holding one of the most beautiful babies I had ever seen, its face puckered and tears running down its soft cheeks.

'Who are you?' asked Jake boldly.

'Are you the children I saw from the window?' Her voice was frail and her smile loving.

'Yes,' I said. 'What's the matter?'

'The baby's crying.'

Is that all? I wondered. I felt a creeping uneasiness. Surely she couldn't have beckoned us all the way up here just for that.

'I can't stop him.'

'Give him to me,' I said.

'That's nice.' And the old lady passed the baby into my arms.

'Aah!' I cried out in shock.

'What's the matter?' asked Jake anxiously.

'It's just the baby's so cold,' I replied. But even so, he nestled up to me quite happily.

'What's his name?' I asked the old lady.

'Wolf,' she said.

I froze. 'Wolf?'

'It *is* a trap,' yelled Jake. 'Look – she's changing.'

The baby squirmed in my arms and from downstairs I could hear an orchestra playing dance music.

Jake and I stared at each other in horror. The baby suddenly felt warm, and when I looked down it had changed into a small wolf, still curled up in my arms but with a wicked grin and very sharp teeth. I heard a howl and saw the old lady was now down on all fours, grinning and licking her lips.

I dropped the baby wolf and Jake and I backed away to the door.

'Run,' he said.

We turned, hurried through the sliding door and, in single file, sped down the narrow corridor. After a while I realized that there was no sign of pursuit – although the sound of music was considerably louder than before. The orchestra was playing a waltz and I was sure I could hear the shuffling of many paws.

'How do we get past them?' I asked.

Jake didn't reply.

'How do we – Jake?' I turned to see that I was being followed by a wolf.

He grinned up at me and I pinched my own skin to make sure that I was still there. I was. But Jake wasn't himself.

'Jake!'

There came a kind of whining sound in return.

'Jake. You must speak to me.'

Again the whining. What was I to do? Was Jake gone for ever? Tears sprang to my eyes and I felt sick with fear and loathing.

'We've got to get out, Jake.'

To my surprise, the wolf nodded.

'You're still there, Jake. You still understand. Don't you?'

The wolf nodded again.

'OK. Follow me. There must be a back way out some-where.'

The corridor broadened out again but there were no doors leading off it, and to my horror I suddenly realized we were back at the grand staircase. It was full of wolves, dressed as beautifully as before, standing on their hind legs drinking champagne and dancing in the hallway. I paused, with my wolf brother behind me, not knowing what to do. As I did so, one of the wolves on the staircase gave a menacing howl and then another. Almost at once the music stopped playing, more wolves crowded out and they all began to clap their paws in what seemed like a sinister welcome. Then I realized the welcome was for Jake and not for me.

Jake bounded past me, and the orchestra struck up again from a side room. He grabbed a wolf dressed in an elegant ball-gown and spun her into the crowd. I lost sight of him completely and stood there, helplessly calling his name, and then in desperation screaming it at the top of my voice. But everybody ignored me and soon I felt quite frantic, unable to identify my brother amongst so many wolves, certain now that he was dressed as they were and that I'd lost him for ever.

'Stop,' I cried over and over again as they spun so elegantly around me in the grand hallway. The ice had gone, the furnishings were back and everything was warm and luxurious. Food groaned on trolleys, liveried wolf-servants stood everywhere. Then above the music I heard the peeling of laughter – and I saw the old lady standing with the baby on the top step of the staircase. She was back in human form, as was the baby, who was no longer crying but chuckling and wriggling in her arms.

'Why not me?' I shouted up the staircase. 'Why not me?'

I could dimly hear her frail old voice above the music. 'You'll have to wait your turn.'

'Let him go.'

'He's transformed now.'

'Let him go! Now!'

But she simply laughed and the baby gurgled. Then I felt a touch on my shoulder. Turning, I saw a wolf in an ermine robe. He bowed low and offered me his paw. The old lady's voice was suddenly shrill with anger. 'No!'

But the wolf had grabbed me and spun me off into the midst of the dance.

'No!' screamed the old lady. 'Leave her alone.'

But the wolf still spun me round and round and into the room with the orchestra, which was furnished even more sumptuously, and the banquet, which was beautifully laid out on two long tables, even more magnificent.

Then, as we danced, something amazing happened. In front of my eyes the wolf changed into human form and I found I was dancing with a young boy.

'Who are you?' I gasped.

'Peter. They think I was killed in an avalanche years ago, but I was lured in by *her*.'

'The old lady?'

'She's some kind of sorceress. Everyone else here used to be human.'

'You mean – all the wolves?'

'Yes, she lured us all here.'

'Why?'

'She hates humans. I think they burnt her mother as a witch, and she's never forgiven them. Not just the Bulgarians, but anyone.'

'But you've changed back.'

'Yes, by dancing with you.'

'You mean – I could change everyone?' I said with sudden hope. 'Change everyone and find my brother?'

'No.' His voice was sombre.

'Why not?'

'Because they've been waiting too long. Their human forms are too frail. They'll die –'

'But you –'

'I haven't long,' he said quietly, and I could feel the strength fading from his strong arms as we danced. 'I don't care if I die. I don't want to be part of her kingdom. Not any longer.'

Then a terrible thought struck me. 'Jake – he'll die too?'

'Not if you get to him fast. Now!'

'Where is he?'

'I can identify him. Come with me.'

He steered me through a pack of dancers, and as he did so the music seemed to swell.

'Here he is.'

He took the arm of a wolf dressed in a stylish blue tunic and pulled him over to me. He seemed reluctant to come.

'Dance with him.'

'But what about you?'

'Don't worry.' Peter's voice was faint and he staggered slightly. 'Dance with him now! Quick – before it's too late.'

He pushed me into the wolf's arms, and we began to dance slowly and then more and more quickly as the music speeded up. We spun round and round, and as we did so the wolf in my arms began to change back into Jake – until he was all there, looking amazed. It was only when he was whole again that the orchestra stopped.

'What are we doing this for?' he gasped.

'It's a long story,' I told him.

'Who are you?' asked Jake as Peter limped towards us.

'Don't ask now,' I said.

'You must go.' Peter's voice was very weak. 'She's coming down the stairs. I can feel her presence. You must go.'

We hurried into the hallway and one of the wolves threw open the great iron-studded wooden door just as the old lady descended the stairs. Both her face and that of the baby were contorted with a terrible rage. As she walked, icicles formed on the ceiling behind her and crept down the walls whilst, once again, the glitter and the dazzle of the furnishings faded.

We were just running through the door and on to the drawbridge, when I looked back to see her standing on the bottom step with the great hall behind her now just one vast, icy, empty cavern. There was no sign of the wolves or the orchestra, and the windows, although still lit, showed only cold emptiness. Only one creature, barely moving, lay at her feet. It was Peter.

Quickly we grabbed our skis, snapped them on and sped off into the snow, but I knew in my heart of hearts that she was still there and she was still powerful, and she and her castle were waiting to trap other innocent skiers and turn them into wolves.

Tim shivered as he stared into the darkness at Liz and Jake. 'You going back to Bulgaria again?' he asked.

'Maybe,' said Jake. 'But we won't be doing any night skiing.'

There was a long silence until Steven said, 'I've never done any night skiing but I have caught the wrong night bus.'

'Where did it go?' asked Liz.

'To a graveyard,' he replied.

4

THE WRONG BUS

I'm not allowed to travel on buses on my own; they say
I'm too young. Of course I could do it easily enough,
but they still won't let me. But when Gran was taken ill
– nothing serious really, just one of her dizzy spells – old
Mrs Tideman put me on the bus herself. She was a bit
confused, but at least *she* didn't think I was too young.
Normally Gran picks me up from my parents and brings
me back on the 92. But that night I went home alone on
the 92. Except it wasn't the 92 at all. It was really the 77.
The driver had forgotten to alter the blind on his turn-
around and of course poor Mrs Tideman never asked if
it was OK. She just assumed it was. Actually it was a
total disaster, for the 77 didn't go near my home at all;
it went to the city cemetery.

Of course, now I look back on it, I see that it was
deliberate and perhaps I was a bit dim to fall for it. For a
start, the driver was a bit odd. He had his coat buttoned
up and a cap pulled down hard over his eyes; I'd never
recognize him again. Another strange thing – the bus
was empty and it didn't stop at any bus-stops at all,
despite the fact that there were people queuing up, but
maybe they didn't want the 77.

I was only sure it must be the wrong bus when we
arrived at the cemetery and it pulled into a lay-by beside
all the tombs and graves. It was a winter evening and
quite spooky but I wasn't scared – not yet anyway – so I
put down my comic and shouted up to the driver,

'You're meant to be a 92. The 92 doesn't come this way.'

'77,' was his mumbled reply.

'92,' I repeated crossly. 'It was on the front.'

'77,' was all he would say, again.

'So I'm on the wrong bus then?' I probed indignantly.

'Can't help that.'

'What shall I do?' I felt a stab of fear somewhere inside me.

'We'll be going back soon.'

'Where?' I asked anxiously.

'Preston Street,' he said grudgingly and huddled over his wheel, hunching deeper and deeper into himself.

Preston Street was where I had got on so I immediately felt better. 'How long?' I asked, but there was no reply and I sat back in my seat, trying to keep warm in the frosty twilight.

I must have dozed off because when I opened my eyes there was a queue at the bus-stop. A very orderly queue – in fact so orderly that they hardly moved at all and in the glare of the lamplight they all looked very pale. Suddenly everything clicked into place: it was Hallowe'en and obviously they were all going to a fancy-dress party. I rubbed at the dirty bus window and looked at them more closely, noticing that they were all wearing winding-sheets. I knew what those were because my gran was always going on about them. 'I'll be in my winding-sheet soon,' she would tell all and sundry, 'then no one will have to worry about me any more.' I had asked Mum what a winding-sheet was and she had told me that it was the thing the dead were wrapped up in. 'Grave clothes,' she had said.

Well, I didn't think much of their fancy dress, it

wasn't scary enough, and some of the winding-sheets looked like they were really quite mouldy. With the cemetery behind them they certainly appeared pale enough, but didn't seem authentic – just a bunch of people badly dressed up.

I looked at my watch. It was only half-four and our own Hallowe'en party didn't start until half-seven, so I had plenty of time – provided the bus started up soon, which I was sure it would. After all, it must have some kind of timetable to keep to.

I thought about my costume; I was going to the party as a vampire and I was going to look much better than the miserable bunch in the bus queue, all dressed the same. Perhaps they went to the same office or something, but none of them was going to win the competition for the best costume. And they didn't seem to be looking forward to their evening, for no one was speaking to anyone and somehow I didn't reckon they were going to have much fun.

Soon I began to feel really impatient. When was this bunch getting on? Why were they waiting? I peered out at them crossly and I saw that at the very back of the queue there was a woman with a girl of about my own age. They were both wearing mouldy-looking winding-sheets like everyone else.

'When are we going?' I asked the driver.

There was no reply.

'I *said* – when are we going?' I yelled at him.

'All right. No need to shout.'

'*Are* we going soon?'

'When we're full.'

'How long will that be?'

'Another five minutes – when they're all open.'

'Open?'

'Yeah. Open.'

What would be open, I wondered. I glanced impatiently out of the window again. Someone was just coming out of the cemetery, also wearing a mouldy-looking winding-sheet. How many more of this office party were going to turn up? And why didn't anyone speak to anyone else?

Then my eyes were suddenly riveted on something moving in the cemetery – just behind the gate. My heart almost leapt into my mouth and I felt a terrible lurch in my stomach. The lid of one of the largest tombs just inside the fence was opening up and two old people were climbing out of it. Unbelievably, they too were wearing mouldy winding-sheets. What was this – some kind of joke? If so, no one was laughing, least of all the sombre bus driver.

As the old couple walked slowly and stiffly to join the queue the driver opened the automatic door, letting in a blast of cold air. He then turned to the first in the queue and said, 'It's the usual routine, ladies and gentlemen. I'll read the list, and you come aboard when your name's called. Right?'

'Very well.' The voice outside was hoarse and dry.

'Off we go now. Ernest and Ellen Petherington.'

'Present,' they chorused together. They climbed stiffly aboard and with them came a horrible earthy, dusty, rotting-garbage kind of smell.

'Nancy Clinton.'

'Present.' Her voice was also dry and dusty.

'Abraham and Letitia Brown.'

'Present.'

'Alice Repton.'

'Present.'

I sat there in silence, still dazed by the opening of the tomb. Then I thought of something: maybe it was all part of the party – maybe the party had already happened in another part of the graveyard and the guests were going on somewhere. Didn't they do that in Mexico? Wasn't it called The Day of the Dead? I remembered seeing pictures in a school book where Mexicans gathered in the cemetery and put flowers around the graves and all the children had sweets in the shape of skeletons and skulls.

'Arnold Pargeter.'

'Present.'

'Annie and Ebenezer Cotton.'

'Present.'

The smell was getting worse and it was so cold that I could hardly bear it.

'You sit there, Ellie. I'll sit behind you,' said yet another dusty voice, and in seconds the girl of about my own age had sat down next to me.

'Going far?' I asked.

There was no reply and she just gazed straight ahead.

'What was the party like?'

Still no reply.

'Where do you live?'

'The grave,' she replied, and there wasn't a spark of humour in her voice.

'Don't be daft. What was the party like?' I insisted impatiently.

'If you don't believe me, feel this.' She gave me her hand and I cried out in pain, for it was ice-cold. '*Now* do you believe me?'

I was suddenly terrified. If it wasn't a party, what on earth was it? 'Where are you going?' I stuttered.

'We're going to warm ourselves by the fires of the living. We're allowed to – once a year – on Hallowe'en.'

'How do you do that?' I gasped, completely bewildered, the cold terror taking a real grip on me.

'Oh, we visit our families.'

'Can they see you?' I asked frantically.

'Of course not.'

'So why can I?'

'You came on the bus. That's why you can see us. It's the wrong bus.'

'Wrong?'

'For you. For the living. You shouldn't be on it.'

'So – you *are* dead,' I whispered.

'I was killed in a riding accident.'

'And you've been coming out once every year, on Hallowe'en – like this?'

'Yes.'

'Is that your mother behind us?'

'No, she's a lady who looks after me. She's on her own too.'

'So you've got no one?'

'I wish I could find my mum and dad,' she said with a sudden sob in her distant, dusty voice. 'They must be buried around here. Nathanial Edmunds told me he saw them last Hallowe'en.' She began to weep huskily. 'I'm so lonely, I want to be with them.'

'Where *is* Nathanial Edmunds?' I asked, a shred of my confidence returning. 'I'll go and ask him – I'll help you find your parents.'

'He's down the end of the bus.'

'But can he see me?' I asked nervously, all my fears surging back.

'I'm sure you'll be able to reach him – if you try hard enough.'

'Wait a minute,' I said slowly. 'You mean none of these people can see me?'

'Just as a blur – a kind of unidentified presence.' She turned round to me again and, despite her grey pallor, her smile was warm and friendly. She had a small, round face and a snub nose. 'My name's Ellie Eves – what's yours?'

'Steven – Steven Shaw.' I rose shakily to my feet. 'I'd better go and speak to Nathanial. I'll find your parents for you, somehow, even if he can't tell me much.'

Ellie gave me the ghost of a smile and I was able to imagine what her smile would have been like when she was alive.

The further I walked down the bus, the colder it got; a kind of icy mist hung round the occupant of each seat. No one was speaking or even turning to each other; they all stared straight ahead. Their eyes were like black coals and their lips were blue.

'Nathanial Edmunds,' I whispered. There was no reply so I tried again. 'Nathanial Edmunds.' There was still no reply so I bellowed the name this time, and a thin whisper of a voice returned.

'Who wants him?'

'Steven Shaw.'

'Why do you contact the dead?'

'On behalf of a friend.'

'Who do you speak for?'

'Ellie Eves.'

The mist was so thick that it was difficult to know who I was speaking to. Then I realized I was addressing a very old man with a wizened, crumpled face, in the very back seat of all.

'Ah – the little girl.' There was a softer note in his dead tone.

'You met her parents and she wants to join them. She's lonely in the cemetery without them. Do you know where they are by any chance?' I asked hesitantly, shivering in the intense cold that he radiated.

'All I can remember is they said it was a graveyard surrounded by oak trees.'

'I know where that is – it's near my school. I could take her there now.'

'It won't be so easy,' said the old man gloomily. 'She won't have permission to be buried there. There are the Guardians.'

'Who are they?' I asked uneasily.

'Each graveyard or cemetery has its Guardians,' he explained. 'They are the Appointed Dead.'

'The Appointed Dead?' I repeated. 'What do they *do*?'

He cleared his dead throat – a harsh, dry, crackling sound. 'The Appointed Dead have been elected to ensure the calmness and silence of whichever graveyard or cemetery they have been put in charge of. But they have other responsibilities – to keep away vengeful spirits for instance, or grave-robbers, or intruders.' Suddenly he stared up at me and his eyes blazed red. 'And you are an intruder. You should leave well alone.' And he turned away.

'We're almost in the town centre now,' I told Ellie when I rejoined her.

'What did he say?'

'He told me the graveyard where your parents are is surrounded by oak trees – and I know where that is. It's at St Luke's Church, and it's near my school.'

Her dead eyes shone. 'That's wonderful.'

'But there are some drawbacks.'

I told her what Nathanial Edmunds had told me, and she laughed mockingly.

'Are you going to take any notice of him?'

'No.'

'Or the Guardians?'

'No,' I replied triumphantly.

'Then you'll take me?'

'You bet I will,' I replied, but despite my brave words I felt absolutely terrified.

When the bus stopped, the dead began to file off and Ellie turned round to the lady behind and began to explain what she was going to do. To me, their voices were a dusty blur, but I saw the lady shake her head a couple of times, and Ellie nod vigorously. In the end, the lady rose and walked soundlessly and coldly out with the others, leaving Ellie and me on our own.

'Are you ready to lead me to St Luke's?' she asked.

I nodded apprehensively and we followed the others out. As I passed the driver I suddenly asked, 'Why did you allow *me* on board?' But he just turned away.

'How far is it?' Ellie asked me excitedly.

'Just a couple of streets down,' I replied, looking over my shoulder uneasily.

Walking down the darkened street with her, Ellie seemed much less substantial than she had been before – a little grey wraith beside me. The thought of her permanent loneliness helped me to crush my fears.

Eventually we arrived at St Luke's, a little country churchyard just on the edge of town which was surrounded by oak trees.

'What was your parents' surname again?'

'Eves.'

Anxiously I began to search the headstones but had no luck for a while, until eventually I saw the names – *Wilfred Eves, 1890–1969, and Edwina Eves, his dearly beloved Wife, 1894–1971. Rest in Peace.* Those must be Ellie's parents, I thought, but when I turned round, she'd disappeared.

Where on earth could she have gone, I wondered, in panicking frustration. Then I heard a low voice calling.

'Steven.'

'Where are you?'

'Behind the wheelbarrow.'

I ran over to her and there she was, grey and insubstantial, her winding-sheet grubbier than ever, crouched pathetically under the wheelbarrow.

'What are you doing? I've found your parents,' I hissed.

'I saw one of the Guardians – one of the Appointed Dead.'

'Wait a minute. Let me think.' I thought desperately, but nothing came into my mind. I felt numb with terror, but knew that I'd never forgive myself if I deserted Ellie now. 'Can't *I* contact your parents?' I said at last. 'Let them know you're here.'

'All right – take this ring. I was buried with it on. It is one my parents gave me when I was christened.' She pulled the ring off her middle finger and handed it to me. It was so cold that I nearly dropped it.

'What do I do with it?'

'Hold it up above the grave and say my name.'

'They'll hear?'

'They'll know.'

The moon was full and bright as I stood above the grave of Ellie's parents. Trembling, I looked at my watch and saw that it was already six o'clock. What would my *own* parents think? Surely by now they'd be dreadfully worried? Then I remembered that Gran had told them we might go and have tea at my friend Sam's, and I breathed a sigh of relief; that was one problem out of the way, at least for a while.

'Mr and Mrs Eves,' I called softly. 'Ellie's here – and this is her ring. Can you hear me? She wants to come and be with you. She's very lonely in her cemetery. Can you hear me? Can you see her ring?' I held it up and saw the ring glinting in the moonlight. 'Ellie's here,' I repeated. 'She wants you.'

'Does she now?' croaked a dry voice, and I wheeled round to see the wraith of a woman in a winding-sheet.

She towered above me and her smile was malicious and evil.

'How dare you interfere in the affairs of the dead!' she snarled.

'I'm talking to Ellie's parents,' I pleaded, hardly able to bring the words out.

'You're breaking the rules,' she said, drawing herself up, seeming to grow taller and taller until she towered over me. 'Do you know what I can do to you?' she rasped. 'I can haunt you for the rest of your life. I'll be at your side every day – every night. Get up in the morning with you, go to school with you, have breakfast, lunch, tea and supper with you. I'll be with you always.' Her eyes glowed like dark coals and her tongue flicked in and out of her mouth like a pale yellow snake.

I knew I would rather be dead myself than face the horrors of her perpetual haunting, but then I thought of poor Ellie crouched behind the wheelbarrow, thought of her being lonely in her miserable cemetery, and made up my mind in an instant. 'I don't care,' I yelled. 'Haunt me – haunt me for the rest of my life. I'd rather that than Ellie being out there on her own for ever.'

In desperation I turned back to the grave. 'Mr and Mrs Eves – can you hear me?'

'They'll never hear you. You're a living being. You can't raise the dead.'

'I've got to try,' I said.

The Guardian put her hand on my shoulder and I gasped, suddenly frozen to the bone. Worse still, when I looked down at my hands they were as pale and as grey as dusty parchment. My voice was a husk as I whispered, 'What are you doing to me?'

Her dead tongue danced in and out as she spoke and the freezing cold seared my bones, making me cry out in pain. 'Now you know what it's like to die – and the more you try to contact the dead, the more I'll place my hands on you. And the longer I do that –'

The more I tried to wriggle away from her icy clutch the more it hurt, yet I still had to call up the dead, still had to help Ellie. 'Mr and Mrs Eves – please hear me.'

'They'll *never* hear you,' cackled the Guardian.

'I'm going to get Ellie,' I said hurriedly, and ran back through the graves, panic-stricken. Once again Ellie wasn't there.

'Ellie,' I hissed, but all I could hear was the calling of a nightjar. 'Ellie!'

Still no reply.

'*Ellie!*'

'I'm over here.'

She reached out and took my hand. Instinctively I shivered, thinking it would be cold, but this time her touch was faintly warm, as if she was reaching me from a very long way away.

'You must come and help me,' I said. 'Let's run.' It was only as we reached the grave that I realized the figure standing beside it was not the Guardian.

'Mother,' I heard Ellie whisper.

'Ellie,' came the reply, so soft that it was like the stirring of a small night breeze.

I watched them kind of melt into each other and I turned away, looking at my watch, hoping I would be home before Mum thought I'd been kidnapped or something. I began to run across the graveyard, but as I did so I heard a voice calling, 'Steven.'

I turned. 'Ellie?'

She was standing beside her mother, holding her hand. 'Goodbye, Steven.' Faintly I could see her hand waving.

'Will I ever see you again?' I whispered.

'Maybe on Hallowe'en night,' came the reply. 'Maybe I'll come visiting.'

There was long silence after Steven had finished his story.

'*Has she ever come visiting?' asked Tim.*

'*Not yet,' replied Steven.*

'*Do you think she ever will?' asked Josh.*

'*Yes,' said Steven confidently. 'I know she'll come – one day.'*

'*Maybe you'll see her in a mirror,' put in Debbie, 'a magical mirror.'*

'*That sounds as if you've got something to tell us,' said Steven.*

'*I certainly have,' replied Debbie. 'If I tell all of you, maybe I won't be so terrified when I see my own reflection.*

'*It was one of those dares. You know — the kind you shouldn't make. I've been making dares all my life.' She paused, reflecting. 'It's the challenge, isn't it?' She leant back on her elbows and stared at the group round the fire.*

5

THE GHOST MIRRORS

My dare was against my cousin, Ben. Right little show-off he is. Lives in Taymouth and Mum and I go there every year. It's a run-down old place by the sea and no one goes there for holidays any longer; there're a few day-trippers, but even *they* didn't keep the old pier in business, so it closed down – and part of it has fallen into the sea. It's a weird structure, and at night it looks like a long, dark finger, all torn and ragged, pointing out into the sea. People used to say it was haunted or that there were lights on it sometimes during dark nights, but I never saw any.

Ben's mum and dad used to run a boarding-house in Taymouth until the bottom got knocked out of the holiday market – or that's what my Auntie Val used to say. Gave it up to run a small supermarket, but we still used to go every year. Made a break, Mum said, and we needed it because we didn't have *any* money – not after Dad pushed off.

Ben's a year older than me and I don't get on with him that badly. It's just that he's always trying to prove I'm not as good as he is, because he's a scabby boy. So when he said he bet I didn't dare spend a night on the haunted pier I said of course I would – if he would. He fell right into my trap and he had to agree.

We fooled my mum and his parents by saying we were going to the vicar's all-night charity sleep-in. I'd been on one of them before; they started with burnt sausages and ended up with cold porridge. The vicar played the guitar and his wife sang. She's got a moustache, and the summer I went she had tomato sauce in it as she sang 'When the Red Red Robin Comes Bob Bob Bobbing Along'. You could see the moustache and the tomato sauce in the firelight and it made me want to throw up.

Anyway, instead of all that, there we were, climbing over the safety barrier and on to the rotten boards of the derelict old pier. It was August and a bright moonlit night, so we could see everything quite clearly and we weren't in the least bit cold.

At first I didn't feel scared at all – and neither did Ben. I was quite sure about that, because although he tries to hide it if he's afraid, I can always see through him. But as we wandered on, past rusting pillars and an old shut-up tea-shop, past weird, out-of-date machines, and the faded paint of the ghost train, a little trickle of fear crept down to my knees, and I felt quite wobbly as I walked on the spongy boards and saw the gleaming white foam of the breakers beneath me. I think it was the sight of that as well as the wind that suddenly made me shiver, and when I looked at Ben I saw that he was all hunched up like a little old man.

'Debbie?'

'Yeah?'

'Do you think this is a good idea?'

'You dared me,' I said nastily.

'Mm.' He sounded doubtful.

'We'll be all right,' I reminded him sharply, 'unless you want to go to the vicar's sleep-in?'

He shook his head quickly, although I knew he would rather listen to the vicar's wife all night, with sauce all over her moustache, than actually stay here a moment longer. But he stuck it – just – and I admired him for it.

'Where're we going then?' he said, trying to sound hard and failing miserably.

'Let's explore.'

'*Explore?*' He sounded horrified.

'Find a place to sleep.'

We walked through a deserted bingo hall and then on towards what looked like an old dodgem track.

'Watch it!' Ben's voice was shrill.

'Watch what?'

He clutched my arm and I found myself standing on the brink of a huge hole in the boards, the wicked swell glinting below me. Hurriedly I stepped back; looking at Ben, I saw that he was shaking.

'This place is dangerous,' he said.

'We knew that,' I reminded him, but I felt considerably shaken up myself, for the wind seemed to be howling a shade louder and the sucking noise of the sea under the old pier's girdered legs suddenly seemed quite horrible.

'What's that?' Ben gasped, and I jumped.

We were now standing behind a partly caved-in fortune-telling booth whose unpinned roof flapped noisily in the wind, and I couldn't see what had caught his attention. I looked down at the dead white of the waves beneath me and wondered if he'd seen another hole.

'Over there,' he said impatiently, pointing to the other side of the pier, and peering intently through the semi-darkness I caught sight of a weather-beaten board bearing the legend MAGIC MIRRORS – COME INTO A NEW WORLD OF FEAR. I noticed that for some reason the sign was much more intact than the others and the paint wasn't faded. Then I saw the hand resting on the outside of the door behind it. It was gnarled and old and withered. And it moved.

I let out a piercing scream. The hand was beckoning us in and I whirled round to see what Ben was doing.

'Didn't you see?' I hissed.

'See what?'

'The hand.'

'What hand?' he stuttered and I could see his eyes were cloudy with terror. '*What* hand?' he repeated loudly.

'Shut up!'

'I can't see any hand –'

I looked back; there wasn't a hand any longer – it had completely disappeared.

'Well, there *was* one.'

'Sure you aren't *seeing* things?' he accused.

'I don't know.' Maybe I was, I thought. Maybe the hand was just a trick of the light.

'What are we going to do now?' asked Ben, looking round helplessly. He is tall for his age and well built, but none of this seemed to do much for his confidence. I'd never seen him so scared.

'We've got to find somewhere to sleep, and the only place that's got a roof on is the Magic Mirrors,' I said solidly, and as I spoke I felt the first drop of rain.

Ben looked at me sideways and I knew what he was thinking. The Hand. I'd thought about that too, but I was really determined not to be scared off. I glanced across at Ben. Could someone be playing tricks? After all, it *had* been Ben's challenge – his dare. Supposing it was a set-up, that some of his mates had got here before us and were going to make me look a fool? On the other hand, Ben was a lousy actor. I remembered seeing him in a play at school – he was a right prat. So now he was looking dead scared, I was sure he wasn't acting.

'Come on,' I snapped and began to walk over to the Magic Mirrors. Ben followed me in silence and the rain came down harder than ever.

'Wait.'

'What for?'

'There's someone in there.' Ben came to a juddering halt beside me.

'I can't hear anything,' I said slowly, and it was true – I couldn't.

'I heard something – someone,' he said doggedly.

'If this is a set-up,' I began threateningly, 'and you've got some of your mates in there – I'll do you.'

'Of course it's not,' Ben gasped, and I could see from his wild eyes that it very definitely wasn't.

'What did you hear?'

'Kind of thumping.'

'Thumping?'

'As if someone's beating on something.'

At exactly that moment I heard it too: a sort of dull, leaden sound. 'I'm going in.' He grabbed at me but I was too fast and within seconds I was in the darkened interior.

At first I couldn't see a thing, and then Ben cannoned into me and I shot forward. Immediately I saw them, dimly reflecting different shadowy versions of me. And Ben. Mirrors – there were dozens of them and they were all distorting. In some we were short and fat, as if we'd both been scrunched up. In others we were incredibly long and tall, as if we'd been stretched. Then there were mirrors that made us round, square, short, oblong, squashed –

'They're only distorting mirrors,' I said. 'Nothing to worry about.' But even as I said the words I heard the voice, muffled and indistinct, coming from somewhere round the next corner. I froze – and I could feel Ben doing the same thing behind me. What was going on? At first I couldn't make out what the voice was saying, and then suddenly I could. The words were spaced out and horribly desperate. 'Help – me – someone – let – me – out – please – someone – let – me – out –'

'Who *is* it?' I hissed.

'How should I know?' Ben's teeth were literally chattering. I'd never believed that teeth really did, but Ben's definitely were.

'It's round the corner. Come on!'

'No. Wait –' he began, but I had already gone and he obviously felt he had to follow.

I stopped in front of the last mirror in the musty old building. It was at a slight angle and it didn't reflect. Instead, the mirror was cloudy, almost as if it was a door. I became aware of the disembodied hand in my own, leading me towards the mistiness of the mirror.

'Don't leave me,' wailed Ben, but the icy grip in my palm became iron hard and I was literally pulled off my feet straight into the mirror.

Once inside, the hand vanished and I was staggering about, alone in the mist. The ground seemed hard, as if it was very cold, and for a while I couldn't make anything out at all. Then the clouds of woolly vapour cleared for a moment and I saw that I was standing in the middle of a great desert-like place, except that there were no rocks or distant mountains. Instead there were dozens and dozens of glass domes, and when I looked inside them I could see myself. This time they weren't mirrors; I could see myself as a baby, as a child, as I was now, as someone who was older, and older, and older. In the far distance I could see a very old woman and I was sure she was me. I slowly glided past them in turn, and as I came to the last dome, for a while the mist hovered around it. Then it parted, and with a terrible, horrible, shock I saw that it showed a coffin. Somehow I knew that it was my own.

'What do you think they are?' said a voice very close to me and I spun round, hoping that Ben had joined me. At first I couldn't make out anything, and then when I focused I saw a policeman. His uniform was a bit old-fashioned but otherwise he looked quite normal. I felt a surge of relief and then I noticed the look in his eyes. Suddenly I was even more afraid than I had been before.

'Who are you?'

'I'm PC Rivers.'

'What – what are you doing here?'

'It's a bit of a long story.' His voice was trembling as much as Ben's had. He was staring at the glass domes and again he asked the question: 'What do you think they are?'

'Sort of domes.'

'No, they're crystal balls.'

I stared at him uncomprehendingly and PC Rivers half-smiled, a look of weary patience in his eyes. 'What do you mean – crystal balls?'

'As in fortune-telling,' he said.

'You mean – you can really tell the future in them?'

'Haven't you noticed?' His smile was bitter now. 'I'm sorry you got dragged in. She's been waiting for a very long time, but with the pier being closed for so long, no one came.'

'Who's *she*?' I asked fearfully.

'Madame Orion – the fortune-teller.'

'And – why am I here?' I spluttered.

'I think she took pity on me,' said PC Rivers gently. 'She knew how lonely I was, so she gave me a companion. I'm sorry – I wouldn't have wanted it this way.' He paused while I stared at him in horrified bewilderment.

'I don't understand,' I whispered. 'What are *you* doing here?'

'I'm here for ever,' he said quietly. 'Trapped in the mirror – and so, I'm afraid, are you.'

'For ever?' This must be a dream, not reality. I pinched myself hard – and the pinch hurt.

'I'm afraid so,' he repeated, and I looked into his eyes. They were tragically sad.

'What are you *doing* here?' I whispered, and shivered, for the desert-like place was incredibly cold and the glass domes – or crystal balls, or whatever they were – looked as if they had icicles clinging to them.

'I arrested her. I arrested Madame Orion – and she died in prison.'

'So?'

'I got a message at the station one night that there were kids on this pier. It had just been closed. I saw a hand – beckoning me –'

'Just like I did.'

'And the hand grabbed mine – ice cold it was – and pulled me into the mirror. It was her hand. Her revenge.'

'What did you arrest her for?' I asked.

'She was conning old ladies,' he replied in his quiet way.

'Old ladies?' I repeated woodenly. 'How?'

'She'd look into her crystal ball,' said PC Rivers slowly, 'and she'd tell them they were going to die the next day. Of course that put 'em in a right old flap. Then she'd tell 'em that she could alter the course of events – if they paid her – and they wouldn't die after all.'

'How could she do that?'

'She wouldn't do anything, because it was a confidence trick in the first place. But she told them she'd have to destroy her crystal ball – which was naturally worth a fortune.'

'And they were fool enough to believe her?' I asked, astounded.

'Well –' he replied, 'as they were fool enough to consult her in the first place –'

'How did you find her out?'

'One of the old ladies *wasn't* quite such a fool and came to see us. I hid in the back of the tent – and bob's your uncle.'

It was a funny phrase that I hadn't heard before; it sounded as old-fashioned as PC Rivers's uniform.

'The only problem was,' I said slowly, 'that she was magic after all.'

'I'm not sure about when she was alive,' said PC Rivers slowly, 'but she certainly was when she was dead.'

'When did all this happen?' I asked.

'1956 – that was when the pier closed for the last time. What's the date now?' he asked slowly.

'1992.'

'Oh –' He gave a little gasp. 'You sure of that?'

There followed a long, long silence.

'Anyway, we've got to *do* something,' I said eventually.

'I've already tried pleading with her.'

'You mean she's around?'

'Oh yes, the crystals show her life as well as mine and yours.'

I didn't much like the idea of that; I could only too readily remember the sight of my own coffin.

'I've been to her – even as a young girl – and pleaded for my release, but she's not having any of it – not her. She just laughs and says I've got to stay. But maybe you – after all, you're young – and I don't really need a companion.'

I shuddered. Suppose I had to stay here for ever? It

would be awful. Just PC Rivers and me until the end of the world – and beyond.

'How do I get to see her?'

'Oh, you just think of her – and she'll appear in the crystal balls.'

The first ball came to life with the sound of a baby crying, and as I wandered up and down at least twenty of the domes I saw Madame Orion as a baby, as a little child, as a young girl and so on and so on, until I came to the one that showed her in the old fortune-telling booth that Ben and I had passed, what now seemed a lifetime ago.

'Madame Orion,' I called, but she barely glanced up. She was reading the palm of an old lady and I wondered if she was about to ask her for money. Dimly I heard her voice from the pier that was now such a faraway place.

'Yes. Yes. I'm afraid you'll die tomorrow.'

'Die?' The old lady was horrified. 'Are you sure? Isn't there anything that can be done, Madame Orion?'

'Well –'

'Please. Please you *must*.' She was very agitated now.

'It could be very expensive,' said Madame Orion carefully.

'I don't care. I can pay – I'll pay anything.'

'Well –'

The image faded and flickered. Clients came and went and Madame Orion's smile broadened. Then, at last, she was alone.

'Madame Orion,' I called desperately. 'Please listen. Please.'

She glanced up and her grin was wolfish. 'Do I hear voices in my head? Voices from the future?'

'Only one voice. You trapped me,' I said. 'In a place you created. Along with PC Rivers.'

But Madame Orion simply cackled with glee. 'I can't see into the future, whoever you are. I never could.' And she cackled again as she opened a drawer and began to count a vast number of banknotes.

'Try her later,' said PC Rivers. 'Just before she died.'

I ran up to the last crystal ball but one and cried out her name. Gradually the mists cleared and I saw Madame Orion sitting in a cell, hacking away with a wracking cough. I banged on the side of the crystal and she held her head as if it was hurting very badly. I banged again and again, the desperation and fear mounting in me, driving me to fever pitch. I glanced around me and all I could see were the crystals and PC Rivers standing with his hands behind his back. The rest was empty space. I couldn't stay here – not for ever – and I banged again and again.

Eventually she looked up, still holding her head.

'What is it? What voice is in me?'

'It's Debbie.'

'Who?'

'Debbie Hardcastle. I'm locked in behind the mirror with PC Rivers.'

'Him? I cursed him.'

'Let me out!'

'I don't know who you are,' she muttered, 'but I do know I must have the powers I never thought I had. I always saw myself as a trickster.'

'You were!' I yelled.

'But I hated that policeman so much that I thought and thought and thought, and do you know what happened?'

'Yes, I know where he went, and I'm there too.'

'Are you young?'

'I'm ten!'

'That's very sad, my dear,' she said with a dreadful sugary sweetness.

'Sad?'

'Yes. You see, if you're with PC Rivers, you must be dead.'

'Dead?' I was totally aghast.

'Oh yes. They never found him, so he is presumed dead. I willed him there. So *you* must be dead – so sad, so young. But you must go, little spirit. I haven't got time for you – or him.' She began to choke again. 'You see, I'm about to die myself. I feel it in my bones.' She laughed. 'I kept thinking of mirrors, you see, and how wonderful it would be if they made people disappear – if people I didn't like just walked into them. You can do a lot with will-power you know, little spirit.' She cackled and coughed again, so I pounded on the crystal, seeing that the harder I did it, the more it made her head hurt.

'Stop!'

'You don't know me. Your ghost put me in here.'

'Then you'll have to ask her,' she wheezed. 'I'm not dead yet.'

'Where is she?' I yelled, pounding again.

'She's along there,' said PC Rivers's voice behind me. 'Look in the next crystal.'

I looked up desperately and saw the last crystal, which seemed to be slightly larger than the others. Hurriedly I ran over to it and peered inside. At first it was very cloudy and then the vapour-like mist cleared and I could see a graveyard and in it an unmarked grave. There was no headstone, no cross – not even a little notice with a name on it. Instead there was an overgrown hump in the ground that was covered in weeds and thistles. I watched the little hump in the ground with great sadness, then I saw something emerging from the weeds. At first it looked like another piece of drifting mist, then it gradually turned itself into a hand – the hand of Madame

Orion. It pointed at me and wagged a finger menac-
ingly.

'Why?' I asked PC Rivers. He shrugged and the
finger pointed again – this time at him. When I looked
back at him I was very surprised, for he looked not only
uncomfortable but also extremely nervous. Then it came
to me. There was something I didn't know.

'What is it?' I asked.

'What's what?' he replied rather crossly.

'Why's that finger pointing at you – wagging at
you?'

'I don't know. I suppose she's just crowing over me.'

'There's something else, isn't there?' I said firmly.

For a moment I didn't think PC Rivers was going to
reply, but after a very long pause he said reluctantly,
'All right then.'

'All right what?'

'She escaped.'

'You mean she didn't die in prison?'

'Not in prison she didn't. Madame Orion jumped out
of the police van that was taking her to Holloway.'

'And she got away?'

'For a while. Then we found her – a few days later.
The pier had just been closed and she was hiding out in
the hall of mirrors.'

'So you got her again.'

'No – no, we didn't.' He turned back to the crystal
ball. 'Come on, you might as well look. The crystal
would have shown you eventually.'

Again the mists parted and I saw the hall of distorting
mirrors that Ben and I had been lured into what seemed
like years ago. Crouched in a corner was the pathetic
figure of Madame Orion. She was shivering violently.
Then there was a muffled banging and PC Rivers, looking exactly as he did now, rushed in. She rose to her feet

and he pursued her round the distorting mirrors, their bodies changing shape grotesquely as she tried so desperately to get away from him. Then Madame Orion stumbled and fell against one of the largest mirrors, which cracked from side to side. As it did so, a great shard of glass fell on to Madame Orion's hand. I turned away, unable to watch any more, and when I eventually summoned up the courage to turn back to the crystal, I saw Madame Orion standing on the railings of the pier. She was pleading and PC Rivers was shaking his head, and where her hand had been was – well, I don't want to go into that now. Dimly I heard their voices.

'Please – please let me go.'

'You must come with me. You're under arrest.' He didn't sound at all sympathetic, just cold and hard.

'My hand –'

'You were evading the law,' said PC Rivers grimly. 'Your injury is your own fault.'

'Please – please let me go,' she whimpered again pathetically. 'I couldn't bear being locked up.'

'Come down!'

'No,' she said wildly, and jumped from the balustrade into the sea. But the images didn't fade; instead, like a television camera, the picture in the crystal seemed to track along the boarding of the pier, back into the hall of mirrors. There, on the floor, amongst the broken glass, was the hand. And it was pointing. Mercifully the clouds of misty vapour rolled in.

'OK. I was hard on her,' whispered PC Rivers. 'She was an old woman and I could have let her go. But she'd done some bad things – very bad things – and I was strictly a law and order man. Besides, with that terrible accident to her hand I would have *had* to take her into custody anyway, so she could have medical treatment –' His voice trailed away.

'She died anyway,' I said bleakly.

'She died cursing me – I know she did,' he replied.

'Hang on,' I hissed. 'There's something coming out of the crystal.'

There certainly was. Emerging from the mist was a detached hand, and in its fingers it held a sheet of writing-paper and a pen. Putting the pen down on the desert-like floor, the hand began to write:

Go now. Take him with you.

I looked across and saw the hand beckoning from the last crystal.

'This way,' I said softly.

'But –'

'Don't you want to go?' I stared at him in surprise.

'I've been frozen in time – I could be very old,' he replied uneasily. 'Ninety-six to be exact, in the outside world. Or –'

'Or what?'

He shrugged. 'Never mind. Let's follow the hand. Anything would be better than this.'

I suddenly felt very anxious. '*Anything?* Are you sure?'

PC Rivers nodded rather sadly. 'Yes,' he said. 'I'm sure.'

We both walked to the crystal and then paused. The hand was deep inside, beckoning, and instinctively I knew what we had to do. Grabbing PC Rivers by the sleeve of his uniform, I pulled him into the crystal. There was no resistance; it was rather like walking through jelly. We were well into the crystal when PC Rivers began to hang back. 'Wait.'

'What's the matter?'

'I'm afraid.'

'What of?' I snapped, anxious to move on.

'What I might find on the other side,' he said hesitantly.

But I was hardly listening as I jerked at his sleeve again. 'Nothing could possibly be worse than being back there,' I said impatiently. 'Could it?'

'I don't know,' was his reply.

We came out to the sound of breaking glass, and when I looked behind me I could see that we had stepped out of the mirror I had disappeared into, but now it had shattered from side to side and there was glass all over the floor of the musty hall of mirrors. I turned round, and there, standing directly in front of me, was Ben.

'Thank goodness.' His eyes were literally starting out of his head. 'Where have you been – and what happened to that mirror? You looked as if you'd almost stepped out of it, but I suppose you must have been behind it somewhere. But where? I've been looking all over for you – and I've searched this place for half an hour. If you're playing tricks –'

'Is that *all* the time I've been away?'

Ben looked at his watch irritably. 'Yes – about half an hour. Now look – what the –'

'Ben,' I said grandly, 'meet PC Rivers.'

'Who?'

'PC Rivers. I've just rescued –' I turned round and stopped talking at once. PC Rivers wasn't behind me any more. All I could see on the floor was a pile of dust.

Everyone shivered in their sleeping-bags as Debbie finished and there was a long, long silence.

'Well?' said Tim at last. 'Hasn't anyone got anything to say?'

But no one had.

Eventually, in desperation, Tim demanded, 'Are

we going to go on with this or are you lot too chicken?'

Again there was a silence. Then it was broken by Rob. 'Maybe I should bring everyone down to earth a bit. Has anyone ever heard of a haunted council house? Well, ours is – or was.'

6

NUMBER NINE

It all started with footsteps in the kitchen. I just couldn't work out what was making them, and somehow it was worse because they always started up quite late at night. Mum walked out on us last year, so it was only Dad and me and he was out of work, so we were always short of money. To save fuel and light bills we never used the sitting- or dining-rooms and during those long, dark winter months, we lived in the kitchen. It was small and warm and usually smelt of frying, which was comforting somehow.

I did my homework up in the bedroom, huddled over a tiny electric fire, because Dad always had the TV going, watching videos of football matches unless there was any live sport on. We're both football crazy, Dad and me.

Some evenings that winter Dad would do his other activity – pretty well his only alternative to watching TV – he would go down the pub. I was usually OK on my own – because I had the pub telephone number – but then I started hearing the footsteps. It was always the same pattern and always at the same time – you could set the clock by them. They began at about nine, hammering across the kitchen floor, heavy and hard as if their owner was wearing thick hobnail boots. Then they would disappear into the hallway and run up the stairs, where they'd get louder, as if the stairs were wooden. Then the footsteps would stop as suddenly as they had

begun. I didn't tell Dad about them; he's the kind of
bloke you couldn't. I love him and all that, but he's
inclined to go on. You know, teasing. It really gets to
you and he won't stop either, not for ages. So I kept the
footsteps to myself.

At first I was scared stiff and thought I'd gone nutty
or something. Then because they became so regular I
reckon I got used to them and curiosity replaced the
fear. I could never *see* anything, of course – even if I
stood at the top of the stairs and heard them coming
towards me. I could never really make out how many
people were making them either. Sometimes I thought
it was two people, sometimes more. And did they have
heavy boots!

Anyway, just as I was getting used to the footsteps –
even beginning to ignore them – stones started being
thrown up at my bedroom window. Like the boots,
they were heavy ones, and somehow it was much more
scary. They would start being chucked at about mid-
night, but when I opened the window they stopped. If I
didn't, they went on and on and on. In the end I *always*
had to open the window, partly because I was afraid the
glass would break, but mainly because I couldn't stand
the noise any longer. Whenever I looked out, though,
the garden was empty and there was no one there. I
used to crouch down behind the window and then spring
up so I could catch a glimpse of whoever was out there,
but directly I did so the stone-throwing stopped – and as
usual there was no one in the garden at all.

Unlike the footsteps, the stone-throwing continued to
get to me, so much so that at last I decided to confide in
my dad. I felt so tired and worried that I started on him
at breakfast, which was always a big mistake, particularly
if he'd had a skinful the night before.

'Dad –'

'Mm?'

'Someone's been chucking stones up at the window.'

'Mm?' He was reading the sports pages of the *Sun* and he couldn't have been further away.

'And there's no one there.'

'Mm.'

'When I look out in the garden there's no one there.'

'Yeah.'

'It's getting to me, Dad.'

'Yeah.'

'I don't think I can take it much longer.'

'Mm?'

I paused, realizing that I wasn't exactly getting any-where. 'Dad, did you hear the Martians had landed?' I said suddenly.

'Yeah.'

'And they're stealing people's souls.'

'Uh-huh.'

'There's one of them after yours.'

'Mm.' He turned a page. 'Get a move on, son, or you'll be late for school.'

Because there was no one to help me I knew I had to help myself, so I decided that I'd ignore the stone-throwing like I was beginning to ignore the footsteps. Maybe the whole thing would go away if I did that. So that night I lay quite still in bed, waiting for the stone-throwing to start, and when it did I pulled the covers over my head. But I could still hear the thumping on the glass, and it went on and on and on until I couldn't bear it any longer. To hell with them, I thought, com-pletely losing my temper, and I hurled myself out of bed and ran furiously to the window, automatically opening it. Then I froze: standing on our tiny strip of overgrown lawn were two men dressed in what looked like rags, but on closer inspection seemed to be old trousers and what was left of weather-beaten smocks. The moonlight was brilliant and I could see quite clearly that they were dark and bearded and between them they carried a third person. Slumped in their arms, with blood running down his face, his appearance was so ghastly that I felt quite rigid with fear. I'd never seen so much blood before; it was like a torrent.

'You've got to help,' one of the wounded man's supporters whispered. 'You've got to help – before they come for us.' He had some kind of accent which I couldn't make out and was gazing up at me anxiously. I was about to reply when I realized to my horror that I could see right through him.

He wasn't *that* transparent, only slightly, but there was no doubt at all that there was something unearthly, unreal, about all three of them. For a moment I thought I was going to be sick, then I noticed that the man they were propping up wasn't a man at all – he was a boy; he only looked a few years older than me. I was sure that he was dying.

'Who are you?' I called down, hardly able to bring out the words.

'We're from the *Rose of Tinmouth*.'

'Where?'

'We came up on the beach in the storm.'

What storm, I wondered, but didn't dare to say anything.

'They were waiting for us.'

'Who?'

'Excisemen.' The man's voice broke. 'They clubbed my Jem. You have to help – where's your dad?'

'Asleep,' I said.

'Not expecting us?' The other man spoke now, his voice hoarse with desperation. 'Is he drunk?'

'He was when he got back.'

'Tom Tallen drunk again. I should have known it.'

Tom Tallen? That wasn't my dad's name. I was just about to tell him when I stopped. Something – I can't think quite what – kept me silent.

'You'll be Silas.'

'Er – yes.' I didn't know what else to say. This didn't seem to be the time to start correcting him.

'Get us inside. *Fast*. Jem's bad.'

'In here?'

'We'll go for Dr Vincent. He'll be discreet. Come *on*, lad. Can't you see how bad my Jem is?'

I could and I knew I had to obey. As I tiptoed downstairs I suddenly realized that I was seeing people who weren't of my time – and they were hundreds of years out of *their* time. They weren't real, they weren't even alive, but I couldn't bring myself to think of the word that was beating away at the back of my mind. As I fumbled with the latch I realized something else. Of course, they were the footsteps on the stairs, the hurlers of stones against the windows. They had been trying to reach me for some time – all three of them – and maybe their power had been growing every night until they were able to appear in person, not just as disembodied sounds. They must be desperate, I thought; it was their desperation that had made them come and I knew I had to help them. But I was so afraid.

When I finally inched the door open I was even more scared. They were there, all three of them, Jem still sprawled between them, and I gave a little gasping cry of horror. The blood was still flowing down his face and I could smell the sea on their clothes. What was worse, however, was that I could look straight through them and see the garden behind.

'Don't be afraid,' said one of the bearded men, 'but we have to be quick. Where can we take him?'

'Upstairs,' I said haltingly. 'Upstairs – to my room.'

'You lead the way then.'

'Right.'

They made a tremendous noise as they crossed the kitchen and half-carried, half-dragged Jem up the stairs behind me. The sound of their footsteps was very familiar; I had been listening to it night after night as they gathered the strength to come through.

'In here.' I wrenched open the door and they laid Jem on my bed, the blood from his hair-line still flowing, seeping on to the pillows and sheets.

'We'll be off for the doctor,' said the taller of the two men. 'But I'll just plug the wound first. Do you have something?'

I ran over to the chest of drawers and dragged out an old T-shirt that had Snoopy on the front. Immediately the man ripped it up and folded part of it into a pad, pressing it over Jem's forehead and binding it on tightly with the other piece. Gradually the blood stopped coming.

For the first time I had a chance to look at Jem's face. Through it I could see the pillow but I could also make out his dark matted hair, his closed eyes and his deathly pale face.

'You'll stay with him?' the other man asked.

'Of course I will.'

'We'll go for the doctor. Don't let anyone in until we're back.'

'You mean – the excisemen?'

'Them – and – and – anyone else.' I could see stark terror in Jem's father's eyes and suddenly knew he wasn't just afraid of the excisemen. There was something – somebody else.

'Who is it then?' I asked fearfully.

'What?'

'There's someone else, isn't there?' I insisted. I had to know what I might be up against while they were away.

'Well –'

'Go on. Tell the lad.'

Jem's father turned back to me slowly and unwillingly.

'Don't let *her* in.'

'Who?'

'There's a woman. She's blind – and black at heart,' he added.

'Who is she?' I said sharply.

'His mother.' He paused and then rushed on. 'I blinded her myself. She stuck a knife in my back and I threw a pan of hot fat in her eyes. It was a reaction – one I bitterly –' He broke off. 'I haven't time to explain it all, but she knows we've beached the *Rose* and we're in this trouble and that your father is loyal to us – when he's sober. She may come here. You've to be on your guard, Silas. She'll do him more harm than the Revenue.'

'But she's his mother –' I protested.

'I took him away, and she's promised to kill him – and me. Nell's a really black-hearted woman – I'll guarantee you that. Be on your guard. We'll be back as fast as the doctor can run.'

I listened to their boots clattering down the stairs and then heard the back door close softly. I was alone with Jem. The ghost of Jem. And I was waiting for other ghosts to come.

I touched Jem's hand but there was nothing there – just the duvet – yet I knew I had to look after him. I had never been so afraid as I sat beside the ghost boy who might die – but was already dead – waiting for his murderous mother who was also dead but as alive as he was.

Even the tiniest sound made me think she was coming: the murmur of the night wind, the flutter of a bird, the sighing of the sea, which was only just down the road. A small animal crossed the gravel path, something rustled a dustbin – all, to me, were signs of blind Nell, the mother who wanted to kill her son.

'Who are you?' The whisper was faint and I gazed down to see that Jem had opened his eyes and was staring up at me, his pupils slightly dilated.

'A friend.'

'Where's my father?'

'Gone to fetch a doctor.'

Jem closed his eyes. 'I can feel her coming nearer.'

'Who?' But I knew all too well who he meant.

'My mother. She's coming to kill me.'

'She won't get in here,' I said sharply.

'Won't she? She's stupid, but she's cunning. She'll get me one day. I know she will.'

'Why does she hate you so much?' I asked, my heart thudding so loudly that it was painful. My throat was dry and my hands shook so much that I couldn't control them.

'I went with Dad – I had to. She used to beat me; and of course after the accident –'

I remembered the hot fat and shuddered. But what did I really have to fear? She was only a ghost like the others.

'I'm sure she's near,' whispered Jem. 'I can feel her presence.'

'You'll be safe with me,' I said, as solidly as I could.

I nearly leapt off the bed when the stone sharply hit the window, and then another, and another.

'It'll be your father.'

'I hope so,' whispered Jem.

I ran to the window and stared out. In the garden,

clearly etched in the moonlight, stood a woman. She held a stick in her right hand and she was looking up at the window. I gasped with horror. All that remained where her eyes had been were dreadful sightless sockets.

I turned back slowly to Jem and he must have read what I had seen in the expression on my face.

'It's her, isn't it?'

I knew there was no point in trying to conceal anything from him. 'Yes, but how did she manage to get here, to throw a stone up at *this* window?'

'She knows your father,' whispered Jem. 'She knows him very well.'

'I didn't realize that,' I replied in total confusion. Which father? I felt like saying.

'He's been good to her, but she knows your father cares for us equally, that this is the only house I could come to in my state. She's been blind two years now, and she knows every stone in every path in the village. My mother can get anywhere.'

But can she get in? I wondered desperately. Surely any ghost could get in if they wanted to. I went back to the window and felt a surge of intense relief. 'She's gone,' I said. 'She's completely disappeared.'

Then I heard the sound of a stick tapping on the stairs and the light step of a woman coming across the tiny landing.

'What are we going to do?' I whimpered.

Jem closed his eyes again. 'Pray my father gets back quick. I'd even welcome the excisemen.'

'So would I,' I replied, as the door of my bedroom slowly opened.

Nell stood on the threshold. 'Jem – is that you?' she whispered.

I held my breath and waited; my whole body was

trembling and the ripples of fear coursed over me until I felt horribly sick.

Jem opened his eyes reluctantly. 'I'm here, Mother, but I'm hurt,' he pleaded. 'There was a fight on the beach and one of the excisemen clubbed me. Father's gone for a doctor.'

Apart from the ghastly empty sockets, Nell's ghostly skin was radiant and smooth as the petal of a flower. She was coldly beautiful, and when she smiled I almost cried out in pain, for her smile was the cruellest and the most malicious I have ever seen.

'The doctor won't be necessary,' said Nell, and she drew out of her long, dark coat a knife that gleamed palely in the moonlight which was flooding into my bedroom through the open window. She raised the knife high in the air and began to walk over to Jem's bedside.

'Please – Mother – don't hurt me.'

Her pace was slow and she pushed her stick around her, feeling for obstacles. But there was none, and in seconds her stick probed and found the edge of the bed.

'It won't hurt much, my darling,' Nell said softly. 'I know how to make it easy for you.'

But I couldn't stay silent any longer and I yelled out, 'Stop!'

She looked around her, trying to pick out my position from my voice.

'Who's there?'

'You'll not touch him.'

'Who are you?'

'It doesn't matter. I live here – this is *my* room. Get out!'

'But this is Laurel Lodge. Aren't you Silas?'

'No, and it isn't Laurel Lodge. The house must have been pulled down years ago. This house is here now – *our* house.'

'I don't understand what you're saying,' Nell replied, 'but it's of no consequence.' She advanced slowly towards the bed, the knife in her hand, while Jem remained exactly where he was — frozen to the duvet, his eyes on her, his face without expression.

'Stop!' I yelled.

'I can hear you breathing, darling,' whispered Nell to Jem. 'I know exactly where you are.'

I threw myself at Nell — and went straight through her, landing on the other side of the bed. I tried again, but it was no good. She could hear me, sense me, but we couldn't touch each other. So what on earth was I to do? Did I have to stand here helplessly and watch her kill Jem, even if she had actually done so hundreds of years ago?

'Goodbye, darling,' she said, and her smile widened with pleasure.

The door downstairs suddenly slammed. Two pairs of feet pounded up the stairs — but it wasn't Jem's father who appeared in the room. Instead, two men in uniform stood there and I guessed immediately that these must be the excise officers.

'What are you doing?' yelled the first, but the second was quick off the mark as he hurled himself at Nell, dragging her to the floor and wresting the knife out of her hand.

As they struggled I heard more feet pounding up the stairs and Jem's father and his companion returned, together with a taller figure with an attaché case. He must be a doctor, I thought, as the crowded room became electric with tension. But weren't they all fainter, I thought suddenly. Yes, there was no doubt about it, their outlines were hazy, like wisps of smoke in the air, and I could only just hear their voices. Jem, however, remained much more substantial as he lay on the bed amongst the clamour of voices that were shouting but hardly heard.

'They're smugglers, doctor. Did you know that?'

'I'm only doing my duty.'

'You could be arrested for consorting with them.'

'I came back to see my son. Let him go.'

'Put that gun down!'

'Give me my son –'

'The gun – put it down.'

'I'll use the boy as a shield –'

I could hardly see any of them now – except for Jem, who was as complete as he had ever been.

'Jem –'

'Goodbye, Silas.'

'I'm *not* Silas. Where are you going?'

'I'm going to die.'

'How?'

'In a minute my father will kill me.'

'Your *father*? But it was your mother –' I began incredulously.

'She failed. Father shot me by mistake, in the struggle. There's only seconds now – tell me – if you're not Silas, then who are you?'

'I'm Rob.'

'Goodbye, Rob –' He took my hand and for a moment I could feel warmth. Then it was gone. Dimly I heard more shouting voices and then the faint report of a gun.

Jem fell to the ground, the bullet smashing his chest – almost exactly at the same spot where his mother had tried to plunge the knife. I heard Nell's voice, screaming with laughter, and a long-drawn-out cry of anguish from Jem's father. Then they faded and all I could smell was the sea. Their power had gone and I was left alone.

They never came back, but sometimes, when the window's closed, I can suddenly smell the sea.

'I experienced something that was as powerful as that once,' said Lyn. 'It happened to my brother Gary and me. He's gone skiing with my dad, but I know he wouldn't mind me telling you — although we've never actually told anyone else. The power I was talking about — it's the power of the trees.'

7

THE GREEN MAN

My parents and Gary and I were campaigning to save a wood. It was only a small one, but we had loved it all our lives and it was special to us, and when we heard that a local builder had bought it and was going to build houses on it, we all went bananas. My dad's the headteacher of a primary school and my mum's a councillor, so we had plenty of push, but in the end it wasn't enough and we were defeated.

At first Gary and I could hardly believe Timberdown Wood was lost to us for ever, but soon a big sign saying PRIVATE: HOUSING DEVELOPMENT was put up and a high fence of barbed wire installed all round the edge. Of course, we managed to get over the wire, but we knew, as we strolled around the leafy glades and dense brambles that day, that this was one of the last times we'd ever walk in our beloved wood, and we were both almost in tears at the thought of losing such a wonderful playground.

As the wintry afternoon sun began to fade, we suddenly saw an all too familiar figure.

'There's Mr Jackson,' I said, and Gary snorted and made a rude sign. I should explain that Mr Jackson had bought Timberdown Wood a couple of years ago and he was the builder who would be putting up the houses. We hated him more than we had hated anyone in our lives and we had written him several letters of our own, pleading with him not to chop down the wood and build his horrible little houses, but he hadn't even bothered to reply.

'I hope a tree falls on him,' said Gary, 'and a mighty big one at that.'

But I wasn't really listening. I knew that I couldn't give up just like that. It was so important to us. Surely it was worth one more try.

'Mr Jackson –'

He was measuring something with a small machine and he looked up immediately. At first there was no irritation in his face; instead I was sure I caught a look of fear in his eyes. I was genuinely puzzled, but didn't have much time to think as his fear quickly changed to rage.

Mr Jackson was a bull-necked pug of a man, huge-framed, with his stomach bulging over his trousers. He was almost completely bald and his large red face was clean-shaven except for a pencil-thin moustache just above his upper lip.

'What the hell do *you* want? Don't you know you're trespassing?'

'I just wanted to have a word,' I said mildly, while Gary glowered in the background.

'Push off!'

'Just a quick word.'

'Aren't you the Belmont kids?'

'What if we are?' growled Gary.

Immediately Mr Jackson began to advance on him. 'Don't you give me any of your lip.'

'Just let me ask you something,' I pleaded.

'Well?'.

'Please, please think again. We've known this wood all our lives. Don't destroy it – we love it so. It's alive.' I realized I sounded pretty dopey but I didn't know what else to say at such short notice. I could already feel Gary thinking how dopey I was, which didn't exactly help, but just as I'd finished talking I caught another flash of fear in Mr Jackson's eyes.

'Alive?' he repeated slowly. 'What do you mean – the wood's *alive*?'

'Well –' I was completely thrown. 'It's growing, isn't it? I mean – it's not dead or anything.'

Mr Jackson threw his head back and gave a loud, rather hysterical laugh, while Gary and I stared at him in shocked surprise. What on earth was the matter with him? Had he gone barmy or something?

'It's certainly not dead,' he said, 'not dead at all.' Then he seemed to take a grip on himself. 'I don't give a damn *how* alive this wood is; it's going to die. It's going to have little red-brick houses all over it – *bijou* residences the whole lot.' He looked up at one of the tallest trees and laughed and shook his fist. 'I don't care – you're going to die.'

Gary gave a startled coughing sort of laugh, but I didn't find Mr Jackson in the least bit funny. He must have gone off his rocker or something, I thought, and his words and laughter chilled me completely.

'We'd better go,' said Gary suddenly; he seemed to have caught something of my mood.

'OK,' I said, looking at Mr Jackson, who seemed to have forgotten our very existence. He was staring up at the trees again, and his lips were moving. 'They're closing in,' he muttered.

'What did you say?'

'I said – the trees – they're closing in – they've been doing that for the last hour. I'm sure of it.'

I glanced up at the trees. Mr Jackson was right; they *were* moving in.

'This is impossible,' muttered Gary.

I stared at him. 'You can see it too?'

'This glade was twice the size a moment ago – it's ridiculous.'

'It's late afternoon now,' I said hopefully. 'Maybe it's just the light.'

I stared at Mr Jackson, who had very suddenly gone down on his knees. 'Please,' he said, hands clasped. 'Please go away.'

There was something terrifying about this fat little man pleading with the wood. Fearfully I looked up at the trees again and could see they were crowding in even closer; there was hardly anything left of the glade now. A little wind stirred the dead leaves round their bases and they rustled sharply and noisily.

'Come *on*,' said Gary, but I couldn't move. As in a nightmare, I felt rooted to the spot, but with a choking sensation of utter panic I knew for a certainty we were none of us asleep.

Soon we were completely surrounded by trees, and when I touched one of them its trunk was warm and pulsating. It wasn't hard either; it was soft and there was a rhythm to it – as if it were breathing.

'What's happening?' I gasped.

'I can't move,' wailed Gary. 'What are we going to do?'

I couldn't think, and we both turned to Mr Jackson as if he might know the answer, although I knew he wouldn't. Sure enough, he was not only on his knees now but had shut his eyes as well.

'Mr Jackson,' I yelled, but he didn't seem to hear me.

Suddenly my legs began to move again and I could see that Gary was free too. I was sure I could still make out our back-garden fence through the trees, but their height blotted out what little light there was and it was hard to be quite sure in the dark. Then I realized the reason why the light had faded so quickly: not only had the trees moved an awful lot nearer but they were taller as well.

'Let's go.' I'd begun to run through the tiny gaps between the dark columns when Gary shouted, 'Wait!'

'We *can't* wait,' I yelled at him.

'We can't leave him here, can we?'

I paused. Of course, Gary was right. We couldn't leave Mr Jackson to the mercy of the trees, but how could we reach him? He seemed to have gone into a trance.

I ran back and bawled in his ear, 'Mr Jackson! You've got to come with us. *Now!*' But he showed no signs of hearing me at all.

'Mr Jackson!' I yelled.

'Grab him then!'

As I yanked at his arm I noticed that thickets now seemed to be growing everywhere, and, horror of horrors, I could no longer see our garden fence.

'Come on!' I screamed. The trees were almost on top of us now and Mr Jackson came slowly – oh, so slowly – from his knees to his feet. 'Get a move on – or they'll crush us.'

'Yes,' he gabbled, 'the trees are coming.'

'They're here!' Somehow we managed to get him moving and he began to run in stumbling little steps between the lines of trees.

'You'll have to do better than that, you old fool,' shouted Gary. 'You've got to really run!'

Mr Jackson tried again and managed to speed up a little, but it was like a nightmare trying to drag his solid weight between us.

Soon a thicket engulfed us and I knew there was no way through. We turned back and ran sideways through the trees but we came to another thicket, and we kept on doing it time after time after time until we both knew we were completely trapped, that there was no way out.

We flopped down on one of the narrow paths and listened to the trees breathing around us. Yes, I mean it They were breathing all right.

'We're all going to die,' sobbed Mr Jackson as soon as he could draw breath.

'You shouldn't have tried to kill the wood,' snapped Gary. 'They got wise to it – these trees. They're not going to let you kill them. You've made them really angry and now they're out to get *you*. The trouble is – we've got mixed up in it. They don't understand *we* don't mean them any harm.' He looked up to the dark canopy above and yelled, 'We don't mean you any harm.'

But the trees simply moved nearer until we were squeezed between their trunks.

'I can't breathe,' gasped Mr Jackson. 'They're crushing me.'

'You've got to tell them,' I hissed at him. 'Tell them you're not going to harm them – not going to chop them down.'

'I won't harm you,' he called feebly.

'Louder!' commanded Gary.

'I won't harm you.'

'Much louder!' I said.

'*I won't harm you,*' he screeched, and as his call died away in the gloom I heard – we all heard – the most extraordinary cry, horribly like that of a huge and menacing animal.

'What's that?' jittered Gary.

'I don't know, but something's coming – something big.'

Through the narrow aisle between the trees I could just make out a dark shapeless thing. As it came nearer we could see that it was tall and thin, but all I could make out in the fading light was that it seemed to be made of twigs and leaves and branches and bark.

'What is it?' gasped Gary.

'A tree monster,' trembled Mr Jackson, going down on his knees again.

'No.' I suddenly knew who this was. 'Gary – you *must* recognize him.'

'Recognize?' he gibbered at me, his eyes wild with terror.

'It's the Green Man,' I whispered. 'He's the spirit of the woods. Don't you remember – we did a project on him at school. He won't harm us.'

The Green Man was at least twelve metres tall, and as he came up to us I could smell the resinous scent of coniferous trees.

'You have offended.' His voice was like the rustling of leaves in a breeze.

'Not us – him,' said Gary quickly.

Mr Jackson had covered his eyes. He opened and shut his mouth, but nothing came out.

'Tell him,' I said fiercely. 'Tell the Green Man that you're sorry.'

'I'm sorry,' gabbled Mr Jackson, and he began to whimper, promising that if the Green Man would call off his trees and thickets and show them the way home, he would sell the wood to a nature conservancy project and the trees would be safe for ever.

'Do you mean this?' asked the Green Man and I caught a glimpse of his face. It was long and drawn and beaky and fierce.

'Yes,' wailed Mr Jackson. 'Of course I mean it.'

'You know what will be your fate if you break your word?'

'Yes – no – I won't break it.'

'I will turn you into a blasted oak – an oak tree struck dead by lightning.'

103

'I promise – I won't harm the trees,' pleaded Mr Jackson.

'Get off your knees,' sighed the Green Man and began to walk slowly away. As he did so, the trees moved aside and I saw a broad and clear path that led right back to our garden gate. Pale light flooded the glade, but when I looked for the Green Man I couldn't see him any more.

'You'd better make sure you keep that promise,' Gary told Mr Jackson.

'And did he?' asked Tim.

'If you come and take a walk in Timberdown Wood,' said Lyn slowly, *'you won't go too far before you come across a great big blasted oak. It's standing by itself in a glade. And by the way, Mr Jackson disappeared, just after he went to a meeting with the building contractors.'*

'So he didn't keep his promise,' breathed Tim.

'Talking about promises,' said Rik from the depths of his sleeping-bag, 'I heard about a pretty weird one when I was in Moscow – in fact, I became mixed up in it. I'll tell you how.'

8

TIME TRIP

It was winter in Moscow and snow was piled up very high in the streets. I saw the old priest beckoning to me as I was swimming in the weird open-air pool near the Kremlin; he was standing on the central island of the pool, staring at me, and his face was so old, so wrinkled and so death-like that it really gave me the most awful shock.

I often went to the swimming-pool. It was in the centre of Moscow, only a short ride on the metro from our apartment, and was heated from underneath so it sent great clouds of steam up into the cold air above. My father is a journalist and he'd taken us there for six months. I went to an English school for the children of diplomats, but I always longed to meet some Russians. That's why I went to the pool such a lot – just in the hope of striking up a friendship. Mum always came with me, but that day she'd felt cold and gone in early to change, so I was alone with the beckoning priest.

Slowly I swam towards him, knowing I shouldn't, but somehow unable to stop myself. As I drew nearer, his face, already amazingly lined, began to change and I trod water unbelievingly as the flesh literally fell from his bones until I was looking at a bleached skull. There was a shimmering and within seconds he had gone, but where he had been standing was a great patch of icy water that definitely hadn't been there before. It began to pour into the pool and head straight towards me like

105

a glacier, its colour yellowy, faintly oily. Instantly, instinctively, I dived down under the water and it passed over me, gradually forming into a miniature island of ice. I opened my eyes and stared up at it from underneath the water. Cut into the ice were two words: HELP US.

I stayed down as long as I could and then surfaced, only to see the ice had disappeared. I swam back to the side, frightened and worried, but somehow, once I reached dry land and the warmth of the changing-rooms, the fear inside me trickled away and I began to convince myself that I had imagined it all. A trick of the light, the steam, the mist – it could have been anything, and nothing.

'You look as if you've seen a ghost, Rik,' said Mum when we met outside the low circular pool with the steam rising up above it. We walked through a little park to the subway, our feet sliding on the impacted snow, and all the way, even when we were crossing Red Square, Mum kept going on at me.

'What's the matter, Rik? Are you ill? You look as if you've had a shock. You didn't talk to anyone in the pool who was nasty, did you? You know I told you not to speak to strangers.'

Eventually I managed to calm her down and reassure her that nothing had happened, but it wasn't an easy job and I realized I must have looked really awful.

Next day, when Mum suggested going for a swim again I hesitated. The school was having a few days' holiday and I knew she was trying to keep me occupied, but I just didn't want to go. The only problem was that if I said no, she would immediately think something *had* happened and start getting worried all over again.

'That would be great – I'd love to go,' I lied, trying to make myself feel it was all OK, just an odd experience that couldn't happen again.

It was early on a weekday morning and the pool was almost empty. A further light covering of snow had fallen overnight, turning Moscow into a fairy-tale city once again, with sharp, freshly white outlines and a stillness that suddenly made me think it was almost as if time had stopped. The water was wonderfully warm and I imagined it must be rather like swimming in a hot spring with your head in some polar region.

As Mum and I swam slowly up and down I became more and more nervous. She often got tired, and any moment now I knew I would hear her saying, as she often did, 'I'll go and change now, dear, but don't let me stop you enjoying yourself. You swim on for a bit.' I didn't want to be alone here on this even more magically frightening day; I didn't want to meet an old man whose face turned into a skull and who sent out strange messages in ice-floes.

I kept looking around as we swam, but I knew in my heart of hearts that as long as Mum stayed with me he would not appear. Predictably enough, Mum suddenly said, 'I'll go and change now, dear, but don't let me stop you enjoying yourself. You swim on for a bit.'

'I'll come in with you,' I gabbled, but she didn't seem to hear.

'I'll see you in about ten minutes – you get your exercise.' There was a finality to her words which left me no room for argument, and she puffingly and pantingly swam away, leaving me treading water on my own, willing myself not to look at the snow-dusted island in the centre of the pool. When I unwillingly looked up, he was there, as I had known he would be, but this time the old man didn't seem quite so old, nor so ready to decompose. In fact he looked much more substantial, and there was a quiet smile on his face as he beckoned me over.

'Never speak to strangers.' I heard Mum's voice ring in my ears over and over again. Then I realized, with a jolting shock, that he wasn't a stranger – he was my dad.

'Dad?' I spluttered. 'Dad?'

The features were definitely the same, but the clothes, old and dowdy and gnome-like, were completely different. He was beckoning to me and I heard a voice in my head quietly say, 'Rik – Rik – come over here. There's nothing to be afraid of. Absolutely nothing at all.'

I swam over slowly, but now with much more confidence, and when I arrived I scrambled up on to the island, shivering in the arctic conditions. As I did so the cloaked man with my dad's face raised his hand and the sun came out, and suddenly I was warm and comfortable. I looked up at the clear blue sky and then back again at my father, but now it wasn't him; it was the old man again and his skin was literally withering away on his face as I watched him.

'Dad!'

'I'm not your father.' The voice was inside me again but entirely different, with a cracked, stumbling, hollow note to it. I knew I had been trapped, but when I tried to turn and run back into the pool something stopped me and I found I was stationary, frozen to the spot. The sun and the blue sky had gone and I was shivering in the deep chill of a penetrating wind.

'Who are you?' I asked inside my mind, but there was no direct answer.

Instead I heard: 'You are needed.'

'Who by?'

'You must come. They haven't long.'

'Leave me alone.'

'You have no choice.'

'I've got to get back.'

'You have no choice,' the cracked voice repeated. 'You were sent to help me keep my promise. Come. Now.'

Reluctantly, with leaden steps, I found myself following him through the swimming-pool mist. The island seemed to be much bigger than I had thought, and when the mist cleared slightly I found we were walking through a little wood full of frost-sprinkled pine-trees. I didn't seem to feel the cold any longer, and when I pinched my arm I couldn't feel anything. I was in bathing-trunks walking through subzero temperatures, maybe already suffering from severe frost-bite, but all I could feel was an awful foreboding that seemed to drive long icicles into my heart.

Eventually we came to a little wooden chapel. The old priest opened the door and we both passed inside. As we did so I heard a strange sound and I saw the priest stiffen. What on earth was it, I wondered. With a shock I realized it resembled the sound of distant gun-fire.

Inside, the chapel was hung with hundreds of different religious pictures – the icons my parents so much admired – and candles guttered everywhere. Without hesitation, the priest went to the middle of the wooden-boarded floor and pulled aside a section to reveal an iron ring. He tugged at it and a trapdoor opened. Again he beckoned to me, this time more impatiently, and when I stood by his side, I could see a flight of roughly hewn steps descending into the darkness.

'You must come with me,' said the cracked voice inside my head. I tried to resist but it was hopeless; an unseen force propelled me towards the shaft. I followed him down for what seemed a very long time, until we stood in an earth-sided tunnel, pitch-black except for the long tallow candle he slowly lit. Then, holding this aloft, he began to walk away and I continued to follow, the fear gnawing at me, rising from my stomach to my throat so I could hardly breathe.

We eventually came to a cave in which there were other lights, and as I fearfully followed the old priest in I could make out the shadowed faces of a group of men, women and children huddled together around a fire whose thin smoke drifted up to a blackened, root-twisted ceiling.

'Who are they?' I asked haltingly.

'They are the villagers of Zarlok; they are hiding from the militia.'

'But what have they done?'

'One of them protected an enemy of the State. For that they are all to die.'

'And who are you?'

'Their parish priest.'

I paused. Then I asked slowly, 'When — when were you their priest?'

'A long time ago.'

'Why have you brought me here?'

'You will see.'

'What is this place?'

'A cave in the woods. A tunnel was built to the church because we knew the persecution was coming; we knew that we would have to hide.'

'*Please* tell me why I'm here.' I was utterly desperate now, trapped and frantic in this dark terrifying place, but he simply gave me his slow, sad smile.

'You will see. Now you must come with us.'

'Where are we going?'

He didn't reply, but momentarily I saw the flesh stretch hard on the sharp, white bones of his face until his smile became the toothless grin of death.

With raised candles, the priest and his flock began to walk down the tunnel; it was so narrow that they could only just move upright. I followed miserably, shivering with the anticipation of some terrible event that I knew instinctively was bound to come.

The shadows leapt out as we passed, and the gunshots and the smell of cordite seemed amazingly close in the confined space.

The soldiers suddenly appeared in front of us. They were shooting at random, and the people fell one by one, screaming in black confusion as the candles dropped to the ground to be replaced by firebrands held in the hands of the grinning, exultant soldiers. I threw myself down, closed my eyes and lay still while the firing continued until there was silence, broken only by the sharp rapping of steel-shod boots. I felt a stab of pain as I was kicked in the ribs and knew the soldier was standing over me, could sense that he was aiming his gun directly at me. I waited for the shot, the impact, but nothing happened and, eventually, after what seemed like hours, I could hear his footsteps slowly going away.

When I thought it was safe to open my eyes, I saw the worst sight I have ever seen – or would ever want to see. Dozens of bodies lay piled on the floor of the tunnel, dimly lit by the few candles that were still alight from where they had fallen to the floor. All were still, nothing moved, and when I got up and slowly wandered about I found the old priest lying peacefully, his arms around a little girl, his dead eyes looking up at the roof of the tunnel.

I felt a churning inside, a dissolving outside, and I watched the bodies around me change. Their outer rags dropped away, their bones gleamed; skeletons remained – and the dust. An icy wind blew down the tunnel. There was a great sighing, almost like the high notes of a choir, and the dust re-formed into bone, into flesh. The mortal remains had become recent death once more. Then someone moved and I shuddered into stillness.

It was a boy of about my own age. He stood up, looked around him – and saw me.

'Who are you?' he asked tremulously, somewhere inside my mind, just as a lifetime ago I had asked the old priest.

'A friend.'

He was short, rather squat, and obviously in a state of shock. 'What happened?' But he knew as he looked round, knew that they were all dead, and I couldn't ask him about his family, about his parents, about anything.

'Soldiers came.'

He nodded. 'At last. We had been waiting for a long time.' He paused and shut his eyes, and when he opened them again the terror in them had faded. 'He promised we'd be safe but I knew there wasn't any hope,' he said, with weary resignation.

'We must go back,' I said. 'Go back to the church.'

But the boy shook his head, his long, dark hair falling across his pale, tired face. 'They'll be waiting there, just in case there are any survivors.'

'Can't we go on then?'

'They'll be there too.'

'So what do we do?'

'There's an escape hatch,' he said. 'We can try that – maybe they won't have found it yet. Father Rosco had the tunnel built so secretly. We could just be lucky.'

I had to ask him just one question – the question that had been burning inside me for so long. 'What year are we in?'

He looked at me curiously. 'Why – 1917 of course. 14th February, I think.'

'Is there a war on?'

'Of course there is. Where have you been?' The boy

looked at me in bewilderment, the fear rising again out of his numbness. 'Who are you?'

'My name's Rik,' I replied as reassuringly as I could. 'What's yours?'

'Alexis.'

'We'd better get going, in case they come back again.'

I turned as I saw Alexis's eyes darken, but I could smell it before I could see it. Black smoke was billowing down the tunnel from the direction of the church.

'They've set fire to the entrance – they must have piled up wood – it'll catch the roots of the trees above us. They're going to smoke out the tunnel just in case there are any survivors.' I began to cough as the acrid smoke reached us.

'Come on,' said Alexis, grabbing my arm. He suddenly seemed to have taken the lead. I jumped with surprise, for this was the first time I'd been touched by one of these phantoms from the past and the touch was real – warm and dry and human.

We ran along the tunnel, the smoke billowing behind us, the way leading us relentlessly uphill. Suddenly Alexis paused. 'I'll have to stand on your shoulders; the hatch is just above us.' The idea was incredible. A ghost standing on my shoulders? And yet when he did, I could feel his weight, hear him panting, knew that I was sharing in this dreadful experience which could lead to his death, and perhaps mine as well.

The hatch slid open; he struggled out and then hauled me up. I could feel the strength of his wrists as I came up into the cold, starlit night.

'We're in open country – we'll have to run,' he whispered as we set off across heathland towards the dark mass of what looked like a huge forest.

The shots cracked out just as we were about to reach the safety of the trees, and Alexis fell on to his face and lay still. I gasped with the shock as Alexis rolled over on his back and I could see the great jagged tear in his chest, through which the bullet had passed.

'Run,' he whispered. 'Run for your life.'

I glanced up and saw the brigade of soldiers advancing fast, their muskets raised.

'Run,' he insisted.

'I'm staying with you.'

'No.'

'I'm staying.'

'Run – they'll kill you.'

Could they? I was not of their time so how could they kill me? Yet how could I have felt the weight of Alexis's body, the strength of his wrists? If I could feel all that, could I be shot myself?

Shots passed over my head and as I looked up again I realized that any decision I might have made was now far too late, for the soldiers were metres away. But they were fading; they were actually fading before my eyes.

They stooped over Alexis and very faintly I heard one of them say, 'It's a child.'

'He's dying.'

'We can't leave him – not here.' The man was very insistent and I could hear the doubts of his comrades clamouring inside my head. Then they seemed to come to some kind of mutual decision.

'All right,' said someone else, 'bring him back to base. Let's see what the doctors can do for him – not much, I should think.'

The voices grew fainter; everything blurred and became translucent as if I was in an underwater landscape. Then I opened my eyes wider and detail clarified. I *was* underwater, looking up at a small ice-floe that was travelling slowly above me. I stared up wonderingly at the words etched into it. THANK YOU, they read.

114

I swam to the edge of the pool, shakily hauled myself out and went to change. Slowly and muzzily I put my clothes on, and when I rejoined my mother I was feeling so exhausted that I could hardly stand up.

'Rik —' she said sharply, and looking at her more closely I could see that she was tense and worried.

'What's the matter?'

'I don't really know.' She sounded vague and bewildered. 'I met this man. He spoke English.'

'So?'

'He came up to me and asked me if I was your mother. At first I was frightened and I thought you'd had an accident.' Her voice shook. 'But he reassured me. He said that he wanted to thank you on behalf of his father. I just don't understand it. How could you know his father? You're always going on about not knowing any Russians. I think he must have been a little mad.'

'What did he say?' I asked slowly.

'He said, "Alexis lived. He wanted you to know."'

I felt a tremendous rush of pleasure and exultation.

'Do you know this Alexis?' she asked anxiously.

'Yes — he was —' I thought quickly. 'He got cramp or something in the pool yesterday, and I pulled him out.' The explanation sounded lame in my own ears but I could never tell her what really happened.

Her face lit up and she put her arm round my shoulders proudly.

'So it's all right,' I added before she could say anything. 'He wasn't mad. Where is he?'

'He just went away.'

I looked around hopefully, but there was no sign of him anywhere.

'You look terrible again,' said Mum.

'I'm a bit tired.'

'You were obviously very brave. We'll take a taxi back to the flat, shall we, darling?'

'Hang on.'

'What's that?' She looked alarmed again.

'There's someone by the turnstile of the pool,' I said hesitantly.

'Someone you know?'

'I'm not sure – I think so. I shan't be a sec.'

'Rik – wait –'

But I was already running back towards the turnstile. The old priest stood there smiling. I ran to him as hard as I could, but as I drew nearer I saw the flesh on his face was withering and the bones were sticking through.

'Thank you.' His voice echoed faintly in my mind. 'You helped me to keep my promise to one child at least.'

'Goodbye,' I said, but he had already disappeared.

Tim shuddered as Rik finished his story. 'Have you ever seen Alexis again?' he asked, but Rik shook his head.

'I wasn't meant to.'

'You made that old priest sound so frightening,' said Alison.

'He was at the time, but not when I think about him now.'

'No, I can see that,' replied Alison slowly. 'I know it's wrong, but I'm scared of old people. There's an old friend of my gran's who always looks at me as if she'd like to steal my life.'

'Poor old thing,' said someone in the darkness. 'She's probably only trying to be friendly.'

'I know,' replied Alison. 'You're right, I'm sure, but I had this awful experience when I went to stay with Gina. She's Italian, the daughter of my mother's best friend, and together we had this — I'd better tell you from the beginning.'

9

THE HAUNTED GONDOLA

I was staying with Gina at her home in Venice for a few weeks, and we loved to walk along the banks of the canals, just talking and being together. One day we were returning home when we caught sight of two old people clambering awkwardly into a gondola. The gondolier poled away and they floated under the bridge. Idly I watched them. Gina's home was near by and I knew the bridge very well. It was a particularly strange and beautiful one, decorated with the stone figures of children playing games. I had loved them since I first came to Venice; they were remarkably lifelike as they hopped, skipped, bowled, somersaulted, cart-wheeled and played catch.

It was one of those early spring days when there's no wind and everything is silent. There weren't many tourists around, just the odd couple, and there was such a complete stillness that the poling of the gondolier seemed very loud. Almost mesmerized by the sound, we stood there, staring at them, and suddenly to my complete amazement something really terrifying happened. As the old couple in the gondola went under the bridge, the stone children came to life, jerkily at first and then more naturally as they pointed excitedly down at the gondola, nodding and signing to each other but not speaking.

At first I was sure I must be dreaming or seeing things or something, but when Gina said, 'Look at the statues – they're moving,' I knew it must be for real. Transfixed, we stared at the bridge, but within seconds the stone children had returned to their original positions.

Gina looked at me suspiciously, as if somehow I had caused the stone children to move.

'What were they pointing at?' I asked, and without thinking ran over the bridge to catch up with the gondola. When I was abreast of it I had the second most powerful shock of my life. The two old people had disappeared, and in their place were two children – a boy and a girl – dressed in jeans, T-shirts and trainers. The gondola nudged to the side, where a small playground ran down to the water's edge, and I watched in amazement as the children sprang out and raced over to play on the swings.

Gina had followed, and we stood there, staring. Gina just seemed curious, but a surge of fear was beginning to sweep over me and I could feel the sweat breaking out on my forehead. Two old people had got into a gondola and come out as children, while stone statues had moved and pointed. I looked at Gina. 'I don't get it,' I whispered, but she only shrugged. Meanwhile the gondolier stood in his craft, leaning on his pole quite casually, watching the children play.

'Let's take a look,' Gina announced suddenly. Unlike me she was a forceful person and a natural leader. I was always much shyer, and although I enjoyed my visits to Venice was often homesick for England. Typical for this to happen in Venice, I thought; it would never happen in Bexhill on Sea, where *I* live.

We walked slowly across to the playground to find that the children were about our age, and seemed perfectly normal. Both swarthy and handsome, with shining dark hair, they were very obviously Italian, but they didn't reply when Gina called out to them. Completely absorbed, they see-sawed, spun each other on a round-

about and then played on a climbing-frame. They didn't
take the slightest notice of either of us.

Eventually the gondolier quietly raised his hand. Immediately the two children stopped playing and walked
very reluctantly back to the gondola and jumped in. He
poled off slowly, while they gazed regretfully at the
playground. Then the gondola slid quietly under the
bridge.

'Come *on*,' I said, surprised to find myself taking the
lead. 'Let's get over the bridge. We have to see what happens.'

We ran as fast as we could, but the gondola was
already emerging on the other side as we raced along the
path by the side of the tall, looming buildings. Soon we
could see the two crouched figures, but they were no
longer children. Humped and rigid, wrinkled and
gnarled, they rose stiffly to help each other clumsily out
of the gondola. The gondolier waved a lazy hand as he
poled away and the two old people haltingly waved
back.

I glanced at the bridge but there was no sign of
movement from the stone children; they were as still as
carved stone should be.

'We'll follow them,' said Gina impulsively.

'OK.'

We strolled as casually as we could behind the two
old people, deliberately keeping at a discreet distance.
They said nothing to each other and neither did we, as
we made our slow progress through the narrow streets
with their overhanging houses and constant glimpses of
water.

Soon they paused outside a narrow house with gables
and slowly pushed open the door. There was a sign on
the wall that I couldn't read, and once they had vanished
inside I turned to Gina and asked her to translate the

words into English. She didn't reply for a few seconds and I saw that there was an expression of confusion and dawning anxiety on her face. 'It says "Chapel of Rest". The building is occupied by a firm of undertakers,' she said at last.

I stared at her hypnotically. Then I blurted out, 'You mean they're the undertakers?'

'I think they're a bit old for that, aren't they?'

'So –' We gazed at each other, both wondering what the other was thinking.

'I don't get it,' I said, hoping that Gina could supply another explanation. She did.

'Suppose they're dead – that they've been given some last moments?'

'Moments?' I repeated, knowing what she was going to say but hardly daring to go along with it. 'Moments?'

'Last moments of childhood, when they could run and jump and play.'

'But how could they be given that?' Can we really be having this conversation, I thought, the fear tugging at me, making me feel sick.

'Maybe the gondolier knows,' said Gina, pulling me back into the shadows. 'Here he comes.'

Sure enough, he was walking slowly and casually up the narrow street, whistling to himself. He stopped outside the Chapel of Rest and then ran up the steps and walked inside, leaving the door slightly ajar.

'Why did he do that?' I asked.

'Perhaps he saw us,' muttered Gina.

'He looks about the same age as my cousin Richard, who's nineteen.'

'Yes,' replied Gina, but she was still staring at the open door and wasn't really listening.

'Let's go in,' I said.

'What!' She was astounded, but whether it was the suggestion or because I made it was hard to tell. I can't think why I *did* make it, but I suppose I knew we had to do something. It would be unbearable to go back to Gina's home without finding the solution to the mystery.

'Let's go in. We can always say – that we want a brochure or something.'

'What would *we* want with a brochure?'

'We could say you've got an old aunt who might die at any moment –' I began.

'You think he'll believe we arrange our relatives' funerals?' she said, staring at me as if I was crazy.

'Well, he might just think we're trying to be helpful –'

She shrugged as if to say, 'Well, she's English – it stands to reason she's potty,' and I was suddenly annoyed.

'I'm going in,' I said with unfamiliar resolution, and I walked quickly up the steps and pushed open the door.

Inside there was an empty reception area and a series of small chapels leading off a long corridor. Each had what looked like a marble interior, holy pictures, a cross, plastic flowers and a raised dais for a coffin. A tape played muted organ music. We peered fearfully into each chapel in turn, but they were all empty until we reached the last one, where there were two coffins, side by side. A tall candle was burning on each side of them, and in their flickering light we could just see that they contained the two old people we had followed up the road.

Gina and I stood there dumbfounded, the creeping horror of it all coursing through our veins.

'We saw them walking,' she whispered.

'We saw them playing,' I replied.

'Then who is he?' she asked desperately. '*Who* is the gondolier?'

'Maybe he's Death,' I suggested. 'The Grim Reaper himself, but being kind for once – spreading a bit of magic.'

We considered the situation for a few seconds, gazing down into the faces of the old couple who looked so peaceful and so happy in their coffins.

'They'll be buried soon,' remarked Gina. 'Maybe that was their last outing.'

'But there'll be others,' I replied. 'I'm sure there'll be others.'

'I don't really believe it though.' Gina frowned. 'Not even now.' She paused and then looked at me with a strange excitement in her eyes. 'You know, I never really believe anything unless I experience it for myself.'

'What are you talking about?' I asked uneasily.

'I'm going to try for myself.'

'*What?*'

'The other way round. I'll go with him – and see if I change into an old person.'

'You might be stuck,' I said horrified.

'They changed back. I'll change back.' She sounded positive and excited, as if she must challenge herself, push herself towards the dangerous edge of things.

'Why do you want to do it?' I said curiously, thinking it was typical of Gina to set herself such an appalling challenge.

'To see what it would be like to be old. I could be more sympathetic to old people – to Aunt Lucia for instance – if I really knew what it was like.'

'You mustn't!' I hissed at her, wishing I'd never tried to take the initiative by exploring the Chapel of Rest.

'But why not? It's quite safe. They changed. So will I.'

123

'It's *not*,' I wailed. 'Obviously it's not. We're dabbling in something we don't understand. And they weren't just old – they're dead!'

'It'll be an adventure,' Gina said, the awful glint still in her eyes.

'It would be madness,' I hissed. 'Absolute madness.'

'Madness?' The quiet voice nearly made me pass out with shock and I swung round to find the young gondolier standing behind us, looking more boyish than ever.

'I'm sorry – we're trespassing,' I stuttered, but the gentle smile never left his lips.

Gina didn't look in the least apologetic. 'Did you hear what we were saying?' she demanded.

'Yes.'

'Will you take me?'

'It's only one way.' His voice was very soft. 'Old to young. For a short time.'

'How do you do it?' I said, but he didn't reply.

'Who are you?' asked Gina.

The boy laughed gently and I was amazed to see that he only looked about fourteen now.

'Who do you work for?' persisted Gina, and although he didn't reply we both felt we new.

There was a long silence, then Gina asked the gondolier challengingly, 'Well? Are you going to give it a try?'

For a moment he paused, and then a look of mischief came into his eyes. 'Why not?' he said coolly.

'Have you done this before?' I asked.

'No.'

'Then don't do it. Please don't do it!' I shouted, feeling quite frantic with fear and anxiety.

'Don't you like a risk?' he asked me mockingly. 'Won't you take on a challenge?' His smile was derisive now.

'No,' I yelled. 'I won't –'

124

'*I* will,' said Gina.

Nothing I could say would dissuade her as I followed them both back down the narrow street to the water's edge. It was late afternoon and there was no one around – no one I could appeal to. But what would I have said to them? That somehow Gina had made a pact with the Devil? It was too ludicrous, yet I believe it to be true.

She leapt into the gondola and he poled off before I could plead with her any more.

'The stone children,' I shouted out to them. 'Gina – they're laughing at you.'

And they were. The figures had come to life and they were nudging each other, pointing and grinning.

I raced past the bridge and saw the old, gnarled, woman in the back of the gondola. 'Gina!' I called despairingly, but it was too late.

Gina got out of the gondola and walked into the deserted children's playground, where she sat on a swing, pushing it to and fro gently, humming a little cracked tune. She was wearing a shapeless old black dress and her hair was snowy white.

I turned to the gondolier and said furiously, 'You'll *have* to do something!'

He nodded and beckoned, and slowly – oh, so slowly – Gina came towards us.

I waited in an agony of apprehension as the gondola came slowly under the bridge. As it emerged I felt dizzy, dry-mouthed, sick with horror at what I feared might be true. Gina was still a wrinkled old lady and the gondolier was no more than a little boy with a guilty grin.

'You've got to turn her back!'

He shrugged. 'She took the risk.'

Gina stood up stiffly and took my hand. 'I know where I have to go,' she said in a quavering voice. 'Help me.'

She took my arm and we walked slowly back up the narrow street to the Chapel of Rest. The door was open and the organ tape played in the background as we walked down the corridor.

'Here it is,' said Gina.

The open coffin was ready and she climbed in and closed her eyes.

There was a long, stunned silence.

'*What did you tell her parents?*' *asked Debbie at last.*

'*That she had fallen in the canal,*' *said Alison.* '*It was all I could say.*'

'*I suppose they never found a body.*'

'*No,*' *said Alison slowly.* '*They never did.*'

'*And what about the gondolier?*' *whispered Tim.* '*Is he still there?*'

'*I don't know. It was the last day of my visit and my parents had come to collect me. There was an investigation of course — but they didn't keep me long and we were soon back home.*' *She hesitated.* '*I'm glad I told you — but I don't want to talk about it any more.*'

The second silence was even longer than the first.

'*I've got a story that I've never told — not to anyone,*' *said Abby's voice out of the darkness,* '*and when I've told you, I don't think I'll ever want to tell anyone again.*'

10

THE VAMPIRE

My uncle runs a very lonely petrol station in the west of
Ireland. His wife died not long ago and he's terribly
lonely, so twice a year my parents and I go to stay with
him. Last time they went off for a few days' touring,
leaving Uncle Sean and me together. He's a lovely
person, full of stories, and he knows the wild countryside
and sea-shore there better than anyone.

Not much traffic stopped to fuel up at the pumps,
largely because a huge bypass had been built, but Uncle
Sean just seemed to be glad that the little country road
had reverted to the way it had been when he was a boy,
with all the wild flowers and herbs and insects and
butterflies coming back now the petrol and diesel fumes
had gone away.

But there was one very regular customer who came
every day – a very old chauffeur driving a long, black
limousine with a young boy in the back. A wheelchair
was tucked in beside the boy and he was covered in
blankets, so I imagined he was crippled or ill or both.

'Real gas-guzzler, that limo,' Uncle Sean would say
with relish. 'Needs filling up every day; she can't do
many miles to the gallon.'

'Who are they?' I asked curiously when the highly
polished limousine had arrived for the second time and
the old chauffeur stood silently by the pumps while
Uncle Sean filled up the tank. The windows of the
car had all been wound up, despite the fact that it was a

sunny morning in early summer, and the boy had stared out pathetically.

'That's Larn, that is. He's got some kind of wasting disease – lives up at Shamrock Hall, the big old house on the cliffs. I don't know his parents, although they've lived there for years. Old people – had him late – and they keep themselves to themselves. Proper recluses. They just send the old man out with the boy once a day and that's it. Heaven knows what kind of life the poor thing leads.'

'Doesn't the chauffeur ever talk to you?'

'Not a word – not even so much as the time of day. I know his name – it's Archie – and he's from the islands. Very discreet, very quiet, and probably paid to be.'

'Doesn't Larn go to school?'

'Not him. He's educated by his mother.'

'So he doesn't see any other children?'

'Not one.'

After that, I tried to catch Larn's eye. He looked away the first time, but the next day he smiled. It was a strange smile, a kind of twist of the mouth and he didn't show his teeth at all, but I thought it was a smile nevertheless.

The following day he smiled again, and when the old chauffeur opened the bonnet to check the oil, I was amazed to see Larn wind down the window and wave an envelope at me. I grabbed it quickly and shoved it in the pocket of my jeans, smiling back at his funny twist of a smile and wondering if his lopsided look had something to do with his wasting disease. He was ten, according to my uncle, and he was certainly small for his age. He had dark, rather oily-looking hair and his eyes were deep-sunk, like feeble little coals that were hardly alight at all. His face was chalk white and there were pouches under his eyes.

Once the limousine had gone, I went inside and opened the envelope. A note inside read:

Dear Friend

Thank you for smiling and taking an interest in me. My parents are dead, murdered by my evil chauffeur. He is keeping me prisoner and gradually starving me to death so that he can gain possession of my inheritance – which will pass to him when I'm dead. He takes me out in the car every day so no one will become suspicious. Please will you come to the house and rescue me. I somehow know you can do it. I am ill – always have been – but he makes me worse. Archie is killing me. I've got my wheelchair so you won't have to carry me. Don't tell anyone you're coming, particularly your uncle. He will think it too dangerous and perhaps tell the police. If they come they won't find anything, but Archie will keep an even closer eye on me and my last chance will have gone.

Yours sincerely

Larn Donovan

PS *Enclosed is the key to the side door of Shamrock Hall. Come tonight. Please don't let me down.*

I stuffed both key and crumpled letter back into my pocket and thought hard. This just sounded ridiculous! It couldn't possibly be true. It sounded too much like the plot of a bad thriller. But despite the dangers, it would be an adventure – and life with Uncle Sean was pretty unadventurous. Besides – I needed a friend, and Larn looked as if he would be a very interesting one.

I turned the whole thing over and over in my mind, but I knew I really had no alternative; I definitely had to go. So that evening I told my uncle I was going out for a walk by the sea. He had something wrong with his leg and couldn't walk very far, so he was usually quite happy to let me out on my own, but tonight perhaps he had picked up some of my tension.

'Be careful,' he said, 'and be back by nine.'

I readily agreed and set off for Shamrock Hall, trying not to show how nervous I was.

The house was on top of the cliffs overlooking a boiling, treacherous sea. Turreted, with long, narrow windows like slits in the black granite walls, it was an off-putting sight.

I avoided the front door and went round to the one at the side. The key turned in the lock immediately, letting me into a darkened corridor that smelt of mildew and old polish. I walked as quietly as I could towards a distant light and soon found I was standing outside a small room that overlooked the sea. The door was open and, sitting in a couple of chairs around a small open fire, I could see two people – a man and a woman. They were dressed in evening clothes and beside them, on a small table, were brandy glasses.

I watched them for a while, noticing that another passage opened out of the room on the other side and that there was no way round. Somehow I had to get past without them seeing me; an almost impossible task. After a while I registered something: both the man and the woman were sitting incredibly still; they didn't seem to move a muscle. The more I looked, the more still they seemed, and I began to wonder if they were actually human at all and not simply tailor's dummies. But their stillness made me feel I had a chance of getting past them, so swiftly and silently I stole across the grey, moth-eaten carpet towards the far door.

As I passed I couldn't stop myself stealing a quick glance at them, and as I did so I felt a stab of fear, for even in the half-light of the shadowy lamp I could see that they were grinning at each other in an extraordinary way. I paused behind a small sofa and took a slightly closer look. Immediately the reason for their strange immobility was quite obvious: their throats had been cut from ear to ear.

I stared at the two of them, transfixed by the sight. They had obviously been dead for some time, for both the bodies were very decayed and withered and when I looked rather more closely they looked so crumpled that I had the strange impression that all the blood had been drained out of their bodies. They presented such a macabre, horrifying sight that I was more numbed than terrified, although as I hurried past them I was all too well aware that they must be Larn's parents. I knew there was nothing I could do for them; I had to find poor Larn as fast as I could and get him out of the house.

As softly as possible I hurried along another passage and up a flight of stairs to where I could dimly hear the sound of music. A huge oak door was half-way open and inside I could see a large uncurtained window that overlooked the sea. Sitting in a chair, facing the moonlit, raging surf, was Larn, but he looked ominously still.

'Larn,' I whispered.

There was no reply.

'Larn!'

He turned round suddenly and I muffled a scream. 'Are you all right?'

'Sorry, I was asleep.' He wiped away some red stuff from around his mouth.

'We've got to go,' I said in a panic. 'Quick, before Archie comes.'

'But where can I stay?'

'At my uncle's house.'

'What about your uncle?' He seemed to be having last-minute second thoughts.

'He won't mind. Come *on!*'

'All right, but I must get my parents' photograph first. It's in their room.'

'I saw them,' I faltered.

'Yes ·' There was a sob in his voice. 'I can't leave without taking their photograph; I couldn't bear to be parted from it.' His dark eyes looked up at me appealingly and I knew that I had to wait.

'Where is Archie?' I whispered.

'Down in the kitchen.'

'Let's go fast ' I urged him. 'Where's your wheel-chair?'

'No need for that,' said Larn, and he ran ahead without betraying any sign of physical weakness. I had already noticed that his cheeks were flushed and he seemed to look much better, but no doubt he had been resting. 'This way,' he said as I puffed and panted up the stairs after him.

'Where are we going?'

'My parents' bedroom.'

We came to yet another corridor and ran down its length to a big door at the end. He pushed it open and beside the bed I could see the soft light of another shadowed lamp.

'Come in.' He stood by the door, smiling as I hurried into the room.

There was someone sitting up in the bed.

I screamed and stood there, stock-still. 'Who's that?'

'That? *That* is Archie.'

He too had had his throat cut, but much more recently, and there was blood all over the pillow and the duvet.

'I don't believe it,' I whispered, and noticed with horror that again the corpse looked as if it had been completely drained of blood. I turned to Larn, who was licking his lips, his long, thin tongue darting in and out of his mouth.

'He's dead.'

'Yes.' Larn smiled, and this time he showed his teeth.

I stood there frozen and completely unable to move. 'Your teeth,' I whispered, gazing at them in terror. The long fangs were stained a brilliant crimson.

'Yes, they're very sharp.' Still smiling, he began to walk towards me. 'Very sharp.'

It all came to me in a flash. 'You never wanted to escape from here, did you, Larn?'

He shook his head. 'I wanted to invite *you* here.'

'You killed your parents – and Archie, didn't you?'

'I suddenly became thirsty.'

'Thirsty?' I stared at him, bewildered now. 'Thirsty for what?'

'Thirsty for blood,' he said quietly. 'All this time I've been ill, I've never really known why. But a few weeks ago I realized what it was: I was ill because I didn't have blood. Then my teeth grew and I knew it was time.'

'First your parents –'

'There wasn't anyone else,' he said quietly. 'We'd always been alone here together, so there was no one else – except Archie, but his blood was old like theirs. I want young blood – *your* blood.'

He came nearer and I could see the sweat standing out on his forehead.

'Keep away from me!' I moved aside as Larn continued to advance.

'Come on, don't make it difficult.'

I was so blind with panic that I couldn't think what to do. Then, when he was centimetres away, I ducked and caught him in the stomach. He went down like a collapsed balloon as I sprang for the door. Somehow I twisted it open and charged off down the corridor, down the stairs, down another flight – and then realized with jarring horror that I was lost in the labyrinth of Shamrock Hall. I ran up one corridor and down another, my panic rising, realizing that Larn would know the house so well, he would catch me; it was only a matter of time.

I could hear Larn's steps and see the light of a swinging lantern close behind me now. Hoping to evade him, I ran down the cellar steps, and with a sickening jolt of terror immediately realized that I had almost certainly trapped myself. I crept on down as softly as I could, and heard a scampering sound in the labyrinth of dark cellars below me. Rats! I almost screamed aloud, but somehow stopped myself. Outside the thick walls of the cellars I could hear the thrashing of the surf and I knew I was trapped. Rats below me, the cruel ocean outside and a vampire child behind me. What was I going to do?

I crouched down by the stairwell, hardly daring to breathe, waiting for him, knowing he would come. Sure enough, I saw the wavering light and heard him begin to descend. He was just alongside me when I jumped on him, and as he dropped the flickering light on the cellar floor I saw the soft brown bodies and beady eyes as the rats rushed off in all directions.

We rolled about in the dust, his teeth snapping at my neck and his eyes dilated with a terrible fury. As we struggled I saw an old bottle lying on the floor and I hit him on the head with it as hard as I could. He went limp and I pushed him away from me, but as I did so I caught the smell of burning. Larn's lamp must have landed on a pile of rags, and angry red flames were already consuming them and climbing up the walls of the cellar. What was I going to do? Leave him? Surely that would be the best, the most logical thing to do. But I simply couldn't leave him to be burnt to death.

Slowly and painfully I began to drag him up the cellar steps while the flames roared at us, sending out great clouds of filthy, choking smoke. Somehow, coughing and gasping, I managed to get him to the top of the steps, but by then I was so exhausted that I sat down, leaning my head against the wall.

Seconds later he had his teeth centimetres from my neck, his innocence replaced by wild demonic fury.

'Blood,' he yelled over and over again. 'I'm so thirsty. You must give me blood. *Your* blood.'

I brought up my legs and caught Larn in the stomach again. He toppled backwards, as if in slow motion, down into the seething, crackling flames below.

This time I knew there was no chance of rescuing him, even if I'd wanted to; he was simply a ball of fire.

I managed to find my way out of Shamrock Hall and just stood there on the cliffs, watching the flames gradually taking hold, and the house slowly burning to the ground.

'Didn't you even tell your uncle?' gasped Tim.

'No.' Abby shook her head. 'As I told you before — I never told anyone.'

The door suddenly opened and they all gasped in surprise as light from the doorway flooded the sleeping-bags.

'You lot still awake?' asked Tim's dad. The only reaction was a loud, protracted snore and total silence.

TRAVELLERS' TALES

The Roberts family are Romany travellers, born and bred, but the traditional pattern of their lives is changing and their treasured right to roam is threatened. This is the moving story of a family fighting to preserve its individuality.

Some other Puffins

ESIO TROT
Roald Dahl

Mr Hoppy is in love with Mrs Silver. But Mrs Silver has eyes only for Alfie, her pet tortoise. How can he ever compete with such a rival? He comes up with a bold plan to win his lady's love, involving some clever riddles and a whole army of tortoises. Will Mr Hoppy's patience be rewarded? And what's to become of Alfie?

A highly comic and unusual love story.

JUST FERRET
Gene Kemp

Owen Hardacre, otherwise known as Ferret, has been dragged around the country by his artist father and been to so many schools that he doesn't expect much from Cricklepit Combined School. But when he makes friends with Beany and Minty and gains the respect of Sir, things begin looking up ... even the reading!

Meet Ferret, his friends *and* enemies in this fifth story of the pupils of Cricklepit Combined School.

WAR BOY

Michael Foreman

Barbed wire and barrage balloons, gas masks and Anderson shelters, loud bangs and piercing whines – the sights and sounds of war all too familiar to a young boy growing up in the 1940s.

Lowestoft, a quiet seaside town in Suffolk, was in the front line during World War Two. Bombing raids, fires and trips to the air-raid shelters became almost daily events for young Michael Foreman and his friends.

But gas masks were great for rude noises, gobstoppers were still good to suck and the Hill Green Gang could still try to beat the Ship Road Gang. Father Christmas would tell tales of his days as a cabin boy on the great clippers, the old tramp could spin a good yarn round the camp fire, and nothing could beat Mrs Ruthern's rabbit pie!

OUR KID

Ann Pilling

Frank has high hopes that the money from his paper round will solve all his problems, but the new job plunges him into another world. He meets Tim, with his rich family and his gorgeous sister Cass, and Sister Maggie at the convent (why, he wonders, do nuns read the *TV Times*?) Then there's Foxy, hanging about the streets at all hours.

Frank emerges from this warm and fascinating novel with a new view of his slob of a big brother, his lonely dad, and Foxy, the cat burglar, and discovers 'the amazing things people will do for love.'